Raves For **Alien Perspective**

"In this, his first SF novel, David Houston renders a detailed, logical projection of the way it will be when Earth ultimately faces its own startling Close Encounter with aliens from another world."

—William F. Nolan
creator of "Logan's Run"

"The marvelously structured drama sets up a complicated web of life-and-death problems...

"The reader sees a colossal crisis from multiple points-of-view and in the process has his eyes opened and his mind stretched...

"The surprises appear constantly, and the finale is an amazing confrontation of enormous proportions...

"No one will put the book down unsatisfied..."

—FUTURE MAGAZINE

We will send you a free catalog on request. Any titles not in your local book store can be purchased by mail. Send the price of the book plus 35¢ shipping charge to Leisure Books, Two Park Avenue, New York, New York 10016, Attention: Premium Sales Department.

Titles currently in print are available for industrial and sales promotion at reduced rates. Address inquiries to Nordon Publications, Inc., Two Park Avenue, New York, New York 10016, Attention: Premium Sales Department.

ALIEN PERSPECTIVE

DAVID HOUSTON

LEISURE BOOKS • NEW YORK CITY

For Kirsten,
who has weird dreams.

A LEISURE BOOK

Published by

Nordon Publications, Inc.
Two Park Avenue
New York, N.Y. 10016

Part I

LOOKING IN

Chapter 1

Silence

Pinpoints of light flickered, like stars attempting to materialize, on nine scopes at a communications console. The flickerings were intrusions—static discharges, pulses from the ship's city-sized electrical system, signs of aging machinery. They were not indications of an incoming signal; agonizingly, they stressed the absence of one.

Reno-ol-Oado, communications engineer for the complex traveling world, felt his scalp dampen and noticed that his breathing had slowed. He forced himself to blink; he was afraid that his eyes, fixed immovably upon the row of scopes, might dry completely and crust over. There was no signal, and the time for it had passed.

So far Reno was the only one who knew, the only one whose anxiety, fear and sorrow might conspire to render him unconscious before he could even report his deduction. The broadcast channel was empty. The other ship had to be dead.

Reno felt oils from his scalp trickle down to merge with fluids that broke through every pore of his skin—before his dry eyes closed and he fell to the cold deck of the nucleusphere. Semiconsciously he heard the scream of a woman. His fading thought was: She had no business being here.

Reno's body slipping from his chair told more than his words would have. Every man on the piloting committee suddenly understood; and all of them felt the approach of the same kind of dizziness that had overcome Reno.

Roia-an-Fera-Pere was the woman who had screamed.

"Take Roia to her room, not to the rest station," President Himi-ni-Oado had the presence of mind to say. He spoke to the two men who had hurried drunkenly to her side, her two husbands: Fera, chief astrogator, and Pere, a mechanic of the spheres.

A Guardian network had sensed the ubiquitous emotional secretions, had assumed control, and was doing its computerized best to maintain the well-being of the ship. Himi brushed oil from his brow and, shutting the Guardian off, resumed command. His emotional control, even more than his aura of leadership or his administrative expertise, had won him his position of leadership. "There are fourteen of us here, a quorum," Himi announced. "Shall we inform the population of the outersphere that our comrades. . . ." Himi noted that no hands were raised. "Good, we do not; not yet." He was glad they had voted for secrecy but suspected their motive was temporary cowardice. "Is everyone all right?" he asked as he bent to help Reno to his feet. Reno was Himi's closest friend; they shared a wife—Oado.

"My nerves are steady," a young crewman responded. "I had no relatives aboard the other ship," he added by way of explanation. "What would you like me to do?"

"First," Himi said sternly, "stop speaking of them in past tense. We do not know that they are dead."

Reno said weakly, "We are in the prearranged vicinity and time frame, and there is no signal." He held the back of his chair for support. "They have never failed to rendezvous before, and, Himi, they wouldn't fail! You know what speaking to us means to them. It means . . . it means life."

Poor Reno, Himi thought smiling inwardly, he's such a good citizen that it's a wonder he was ever elected to his post. Aloud, Himi said, "Reno, virtuous intentions by a majority might preserve society—but not the universe."

There were scattered murmurs as several expressed a suspicion that their leader had indulged in cynicism.

"We cannot forsee all that the universe may hold," Himi continued, "and we can deal only with the emergencies within the mechanical capabilities of our traveling world. It is the same for them. You know that, or you could not believe that they might be dead. Perhaps there was minor damage from space debris—something too small to be detected or too massive to be shunted by deflectors. Perhaps some difficulty arose during a planetary exploration that delayed their departure. Perhaps, perhaps, perhaps. Too many of us have relatives or friends out there," Himi said softly, "for fatalism to be allowed to set in." His words carried unusual conviction: his own brother commanded the other vessel.

"What do we tell the others—the women and children?"

"Can we extend our time here?"

"Can we locate them and go to their rescue?"

"What message do we transmit to the people at home?"

The questions tumbled out chaotically. Himi was about to stop them when one officer was heard to say:

"There is a civilized planet around 23-989-6. Do you suppose our friends have been attacked?" And all fell silent.

Thoughtfully, Himi commented in the silence, "We know very little about the aliens there, so the possibility must not be ignored. Insanity might be the norm for an alien mind."

Himi despised the pointless and crippling fear of the unknown; and now he himself had been guilty of encouraging it. He shattered the mystical mood by announcing loudly and cheerily: "None of us are voteless halfwits! Together we will find some answers and select the appropriate course of action. We must pool our opinions!" Himi knew the options already, but he had to allow the others to believe that the decisions had been communally arrived at. He gestured for the committeemen to seat themselves at the conference table.

"Here comes Fera," Reno muttered taking his place.

"Fearless Fera," Himi snorted under his breath. If level-headedness alone could insure leadership, Fera would surely have bested Himi in the Presidential elections. Himi reflected: Fearless Fera has probably never felt any emotion stronger than disdain.

"I insist," Fera said sharply, slipping into a seat at the table, "that any vote taken in my absence be repeated."

"There's been only the decision to ask for a vote," Himi said evenly. "Have you a proposition to introduce?"

"The obvious one. That we go about our duties, inform everyone of what has happened, monitor our scopes diligently. If the silence continues, we should proceed on our way."

The heartlessness of the idea offended the committeemen. "If our friends are not transmitting," asked one of the men, "how can we locate them? They'd be like a molecule in this tabletop."

Reno suddenly leapt from the table and ran to his scopes. He adjusted some controls and peered unblinkingly at the still-empty screens. Then he returned to his chair. "I thought of their distress beacon," he explained, "but they haven't activated that either."

"They are dead," Fera pronounced.

"Are they dead?" Himi challenged. He quickly counted the raised hands. Had Himi not been there, it would have been a tie vote. "They are not dead," Himi summed up. He hastily posed a follow-up question. "Should we extend our time in the transmission range?" Before a vote could be taken, Himi said, "Rald, tell us the course that would most efficiently extend our time here. Dool, when we have his report, compute the additional cost in fuel and other consumables. Reno, could our reception equipment be altered to increase our search capabilities?"

"I ask for a suspension of this meeting while I compute," Rald requested.

After seeing a vote largely in favor of granting Rald his suspension, Himi stretched back languidly in his chair and congratulated himself for deftly manipulating the meeting. Fera sulked.

An attendant arrived with a cart of alcohol-soaked towels which he dispensed without curiosity. Attendants were chosen in adolescence for their inferior native intelligence. They were not educated and generally seemed content in their ignorance.

Several men disrobed completely to remove the uncomfortable body oils. Reno requested an extra towel for his hair. Eyes darted to the scopes from time to time; hopes rose and fell with each flicker of meaningless static.

"If we accelerate at once," Rald said, re-establishing the meeting, "a constant low-yield acceleration without stopping the spheres, we can head toward 23-989-6 in a path that will keep us in range for an additional 43 days."

"The expense would be negligible," Dool said; "but if we coast for the full 43 days, the acceleration needed to return us to our proper path would be...." He consulted his notes and reported a series of numbers that were meaningless to most—except that they left an impression of a great, perhaps unacceptable, cost.

As Reno was concluding his report (there was very little, he said, that could boost the reception equipment), a movement caught his eye. "Look!" he interrupted himself, pointing toward his station.

Lights danced nonsensically on the scope second from the far end. Reno slung his towels around his neck and sprinted to the controls. "It *is* a signal," he said hesitantly, "but not our kind. Just a stray echo. From the aliens of the third planet. A picture I think, but the scanning is unlike ours. The computer can clarify—"

"Don't waste time," Fera chided. "It makes no difference what the picture is."

Reno had steadied the static into wavering shapes. The shapes solidified as he sensitively touched the controls. He had a picture, that of an airless crater-marked plain on an uninhabitable world.

"Satisfied?" Fera asked sarcastically. "I propose a vote—"

Himi cut him off politely. "Let us first examine the remaining questions; they are sure to interrelate." Then, he thought confidently, we can vote on my whole plan of action. "For example, if we should find our people within the nearby planetary system, and in distress, couldn't we actually enter the system, refuel from the atmosphere of the fifth planet, just as they planned to do, and...?"

Although Fera opposed him at many turnings, Himi finally saw the acceptance of his package of plans and options. It was decided that for now no message home would be dispatched; that women aboard the ship would be told that a minor miscalculation had led to a delay in reception; and that children would be encouraged to assume that their pen-pal communications would be just a bit late in coming. It was further decided that an arc toward the star 23-989-6 would be traveled to gain the computed extra time, but that only half the time and distance would be spent in order to conserve re-acceleration fuel. If the ship were located and found to be in need of help, the various rescue-mission proposals would then be considered.

Himi observed a familiar occurence: the onset of a feeling of euphoric equanimity, a drunkenness following the sincere belief that all that could be done had been done. He observed it affecting the faces of his fellow officers, and he felt it as a tingling in his own joints. Fera alone seemed unchanged by the.passage of Himi's resolution. Fera retained his tensions until the vote was taken to adjourn and he literally had nothing further to challenge, manipulate, distort, or even bother remembering; such, at least, was Himi's impression.

When the officers had excused themselves and returned to their duties, Himi quietly slipped away to his private place.

Himi kept a pressure suit hidden in a locker near the south escape tunnel of the nucleusphere. He dressed, unseen, and then pulled himself along the great axleway to the port that opened onto the ship's empty innersphere. As he reached out to touch the work-light switch, he felt his usual pang of guilt: this was an exorbitant expense of energy for so self-indulgent an act as he was about to commit.

His secret world was bathed in light.

Spheres within spheres within spheres comprised the

ship, and Himi was now on the surface of the central spinning ball thal housed the command center and living quarters for the pilots, directors, and their assistants. He kept his legs clamped in a mesh of cables to avoid being spun off. In the ghostly glow of the work lights, the distant surface of the outersphere curved around and filled Himi's field of view. He was like a mammoth man on a tiny planet, under the dome of a metal sky. He "lay" on the "ground" looking "up" at the "sky"—which even seemed to have "clouds": traveling discolorations in the metal.

It was here that Himi came on occasion to refuel his spirit. What inspired him was not merely the sight of so vast an open space; nor was it the complete solitude; nor was it the reminder of home and sky. It was the ship itself. Himi was by inclination an organizer, not a creator. That such a vessel as this could have been conceived and constructed was a miracle to him. That such a mission as his could have been dreamed of and then realized meant to him that man's destiny was limitless. With the ship's totality in view, pettiness fell into perspective; Himi's own errors seemed insignificant; and all things seemed possible—even that his brother might be still alive.

Watching the dizzying motion of the spheres, Himi thought: I wish there was truth in it, that he and I had that mystic connection they used to kid us about. I could send out my mind now, and I could know. Perhaps he too is hiding in the innersphere of his ship watching the clouds rush by, thinking to me that all is well.

Himi imagined that he could see through the skin of the outersphere onto the heads of the hundreds who inhabited the equitorial region where centrifugal gravity helped simulate a planetary environment—the living quarters, bedrooms, nurseries, food preparation centers,

12

laboratories, athletic clubs—all filled with people he had seen rarely if at all and did not know. Explorers, scientists, physicians, librarians—all trusting the unseen team in the nucleusphere to take them safely from star to star—all worshiping, out of necessity—the name of Himi. Just as a similar community worshiped his brother's name.

His thoughts drifting, Himi wondered, as he had before, if it would be safe for a man of advanced years, such as himself, to float loose and "fall" to the turning dish of the outersphere—where he could stand centrifugally weighted and look up suddenly at the ball of the nucleusphere spinning like a planet in a cage of cables. Himi had never done it, but he thought again, like a curious child, how awesome such an abrupt change in perspective might be.

The turning spectacle of power and purpose had done its work. The pessimism Himi had concealed from the others was now truly gone; he had found reason to hope. He fitted himself back through the escape port into the axleway that would take him back to the control station of the nucleusphere—where he would wait.

Chapter 2

Waiting

Children, most of whom had accepted the announced delay without question or anxiety, hurried from various points on the outersphere to their polling place. There they milled about happily awaiting their turns at the voting keyboards.

Two who were thick-skinned, just turned adolescent, were apart from the group and spoke secretively:

"I think they record our voting patterns."

"Why would they do that?" asked the smaller of the two.

"It helps them decide our futures. They must look for certain kinds of voters to train to be leaders. I'll bet they do. I'll bet the lighted switch-buttons register our fingerprints—just as adult controls on the ship do."

The smaller asked incredulously: "How did you learn that? How do you know about adult controls and fingerprints?"

"I just figured it out, watching how things work."

"You're not supposed to do that."

"I don't know how to keep from doing it. My mind just seems to work that way."

The smaller looked up admiringly at his companion. "How are you going to vote?" the little fellow asked, indicating by a slyness of intonation that a forbidden question had been asked.

The casual answer was even more daring; it failed to acknowledge the immorality of the question—as if morality were of no consequence: "I shall vote for an extended play period, for the puppet show about adult love making, for frozen custard, and for myself as recreation captain. And I shall do so because I believe those will be the most popular votes, and I want the adults to know I can sense the will of the majority."

"But what do *you* want?"

"To be a leader. How will you vote this time?"

"Oh, I really don't care. Perhaps I won't vote."

The older child was too shocked to respond—until he realized he had heard a joke, a truly obscene one. Perhaps this bright little friend wasn't so ordinary after all. Perhaps he would not become a woman.

Two adolescents played at tag down an empty corridor. One of them suddenly contracted, doubled over and fell. "Ow—my arm!"

The youth's companion felt a pang of jealousy: his friend's metamorphosis was beginning. The two made their way to the infirmary.

"Was it an air bubble?" the afflicted youth asked the physician, expectantly.

"It was. You're a mite early, Alio, but I think your shell is beginning to loosen. I'd say that in about, oh, a day or so—"

15

"I will be an adult," the youth pronounced solemnly. He looked a question at his doctor.

The man nodded, unable to hide a smile. "It looks as if you will be a male, Alio."

Alio's pride—combined with a dizziness born of almost unbearable excitement—seemed to counteract the inertial gravity of the outersphere; he felt dreamily weightless.

The women's club was on the third and innermost level of the outersphere and out near the north axis—where centrifugal effects were least and one could relax merely by virtue of having shed a few pounds.

Jimi, Alio's mother, was almost alone in the music room: she was separated by a refreshment table from several chattering ladies at a corner booth. She looked depressed. The tranquil music of sustained chords was apparently wasted upon her ears.

"Jimi! What are you doing tucked away up here? I expected to find you turning cartwheels down the corridors!"

Jimi looked up and saw her friend approaching from the doorway. "Aren't you worried, Pani?" Jimi asked when her friend was seated facing her.

"Oh, a little concerned, but I wouldn't be if *my* child were about to become a man. I've only had one come out of his shell so far, a defective girl who had to be—" Pani interrupted herself; she could not say destroyed. "And here you sit like a lump of goo. What can be so wrong?"

"The sister ship. I don't believe what we've been told."

Jimi's words would have been blasphemous coming from a man; but women were so seldom taken seriously that their ideas could be expressed quite openly. Besides, Pani was her dearest friend.

16

"But why don't you believe? And so what? You've mothered a son!"

"Pani, in all our years we've never had a schedule error. Why now? We've received messages they've sent from light years away, and received them right on the dot. Now they're only about a week away . . . or they're supposed to be."

"How do you know these things?"

"My husbands. When a communications expert speaks to an explorer—even I understand some of what they say."

Pani raised her brow in sarcasm. "You wouldn't learn much from a maintenance engineer and a food processor. My two just talk about garbage." Jimi didn't laugh or indicate she had heard; she seemed to be staring wistfully at a cake on the refreshment table. Pani tried again to interest Jimi, this time with an item that happened to be near the top of her mind:

"Did you hear where they found little Llia yesterday? In the innersphere! He's all right, not hurt at all. He stole a small pressure suit. Said he did it just to make sure there *was* a nucleusphere. Imagine anything so bizarre? He's in psychiatric." She gave up and returned to the only subject Jimi seemed concerned with: "Well what *did* you learn about the schedule thing? What kind of error do you think they're making?"

"What if there's no error at all? And there's just no message coming in?"

"You mean, suppose it's their error, not ours?"

"They wouldn't make a scheduling error either."

"But then—" Pani drew in her breath sharply and lowered her voice. "But maybe . . . some simple error! Jimi, you don't have anyone out there do you? I don't remember a relative of yours—"

17

"They are our people, and . . ."

Pani waited for a confidence to follow Jimi's hesitation. The delay was so protracted and Jimi's expression changed so slowly that the shock of her revelation was lessened.

"And there is a man there. Oran-an-Lado. He . . . I never knew him really well, but at Academy when the men first began to choose their partners, I was his choice. He *wanted* me. But there was a conflict with the co-husband and I had to be reassigned."

Pani affectionately pressed the back of her friend's hand then rose silently and left the club—not so much troubled as beset by a need to gossip.

The explorer's club contained the ship's best-equipped gym—located on the first (heaviest) level, at the equitorial (heaviest) latitude. It was crowded as usual. Over a background of groans and wheezes, the men at exercise machines carried on a leisurely, apparently directionless, conversation:

"Anybody awake last night?"

"I felt it . . . woke me up."

"Nice night, aside from that. Say, Nali, tonight?"

"Uhn . . . take her . . . I'm gonna be too exhausted."

"Anybody know what's going on? Hand me that plate over there, Veda."

He dropped the heavy plate on another; the shattering clang made every ear ring.

"Voteless bastard! Be careful!"

"What? I can't hear you."

"Funny."

"Course correction?"

"Vote."

18

There was an almost unanimous affirmative, cast mostly as grunts.

"What's a course correction got to do with a miscalculated time factor? They can't have miscalculated that much."

"Wonder why they never put an explorer on the pilot committee?"

"Ever been to the nucleusphere? I wouldn't want that thankless job."

"Well, what thanks do *we* get? Mino, toss me a towel. Anybody else for alcohol?"

"What's your hurry? Going somewhere?"

"Occurred to me that somebody ought to . . . go somewhere."

"Try picking up the intercom."

"They're not taking any calls from out here."

"Are you serious? Why not?"

There was no response, but the tense silence indicated that each of them knew the obvious answer—which therefore needn't be articulated.

"Hey, don't throw towels around like that . . . got alcohol in my eyes. What's gnawing at you?"

"Condescension. Deception. Injustice. Things like that."

"Want disclosure and a universal concensus?"

"How about demanding a grove of trees and a waterfall?"

With thuds and clanks, they dropped or replaced their weights or machines, one at a time, as each, catching the eyes of the others, realized that some sort of decision was about to be reached.

"Nali has a friend, Fera-sa-Roia . . ."

No society voted as did the explorers. They could reach

19

even the most complex decisions without so much as a show of hands, and within the company of others who might not realize any decision was being sought.

"Support personnel," Nali demanded with no questioning intonation, as he began to remove his exercise suit.

Each of the nineteen present volunteered.

"Alcohol," Nali said peremptorily.

They all stripped and followed him to the sprays.

Maoi, a life-sciences researcher, by several years the oldest man aboard, hurried into the physical sciences laboratory. He was breathless and exuding oils.

"Nali and," he gasped, "the explorers. They're heading for the south lock—" He stopped to take a deep breath.

"Why?" asked one of the three scientists at work there.

"Can't you guess?" interjected another.

"This is not the time," Maoi continued haltingly, "to stir confusion in the nucleusphere. The pilots have... enough to contend with."

"Do you know what they're contending with?" Maoi was asked.

"I think so. I believe the other ship is ... either dead or in distress."

The three younger scientists helped Maoi into a chair. "We agree," one told him. "We have reasoned that they have taken a course toward 23-989-6; we can agree upon no other explanation. And it's hardly surprising that the nucleusphere is exercising caution. I think I would vote for secrecy with them if I were there."

"Why, a full disclosure, if abrupt, would render half the ship's personnel unconscious!" another added, by way of agreement.

"I think," Maoi said, "that we must stop the explorers."

"How? It would take all four of us just to subdue the feeblest of them!"

Ania-do-Jimi had just listened until now. "I know Himi and Reno," Ania said. "I think one of them might accept a call from me. Let me try to warn them that the explorers are coming. If they think it necessary, they can seal off the entrance locks. Does anyone object?"

Technically, there were too few scientists assembled to constitute a societal quorum; they had no right to decide, to object, or to act. But secrecy was at stake.

"I'd hate to antagonize the explorers," one of them muttered.

The lights in the lab were dim. Until Maoi had interrupted, tests had been underway involving rocket-engine starter pellets. The spectrobolometer in use still cast a wavering pink glow against a reflective plate - adding to the sense of unreality prevailing in the normally impersonal room.

"I can convey all our concerns, I think," Ania said, noting the nods of agreement. He switched on the lab lights and let his hands hover over the intercom keyboard while he composed his thoughts. Slowly, almost idly, he typed in the coordinates for Reno's console.

In the brighter light, it was noted that Maoi had absent-mindedly taken two radioactive pellets from the workbench and was grinding them together in his hand. Amused but genuinely concerned, the physical scientists scrambled to take the dangerous spheroids from the biologist. "They're hot pellets, you know," one told him.

"Oh, a few minutes' exposure never hurt anyone," the old man grumbled.

"Have you heard about Alio? He's losing his shell; he'll be a man," a scientist told Maoi as he took a radiation count from the endangered palm.

21

Maoi returned: "Yes, and Rera-Lald's wife has just given birth. And I shall probably be the first to die of old age. The cycles of life do seem eternal, don't they."

A written message began to appear on the intercom scope. The succinct reply from Reno was: "The four of you, come to the nucleusphere at once."

Although expected, the reply was frightening: for the first time in their history all parliamentary procedure was being ignored and decisions were being made without a vote. It did not seem possible, and yet it seemed inescapable. The eternal social structure was being shown to be merely a product of mind: ignored, it ceased to exist.

Chapter 3

The Message

Suppressing their indignation, the explorers entered the nucleusphere respectfully, their pressure helmets cupped under their left arms—almost in military fashion (indeed, many explorers came from military background or ancestry).

Four of the nineteen had never been here before; the others had visited only once or twice out of curiosity. It was always an awesome sight:

Aside from the airless innersphere, this was the most spacious enclosure of the ship. One entered the seat of power via a stairwell that led up through the floor from the corridor below. Ahead up the curving floor, behind up the curving floor, and directly above as if their feet were riveted to the ceiling, technicians labored at machinery and instrument consoles. During this short visit, the dwellers of the outersphere could not hope to become accustomed to the peculiar environment. Walking away from the stairwell to familiar corridors below, their perspective began disorientingly to shift. Up could suddenly seem to be down, or across, and then unexpectedly it would seem like up again; they had entered an optical illusion. They tried to keep their eyes on the comforting floor.

"Nali, old friend," Fera said, approaching the explorer, "welcome."

Nali could not reply. He had known Fera decades ago when they were students; he had visited him in the lower corridors of the nucleusphere and had dined with him twice when Fera had vacationed in the outersphere. But here, where Fera belonged, Nali saw him as a giant of a man, a stranger, a god entrusted with the political and physical well-being of a world.

Himi and Reno joined Fera and the group of explorers. "Are you the explorer Nali?" Reno asked.

"Yes."

"It is good of you to come. We face an unusual crisis, and we have voted here to inform your group and a representative group of scientists—"

"Wouldn't you know..." one explorer muttered to another.

"—of everything concerning our rendezvous. Please take seats at the conference table."

Emerging from the stairs, the scientists seemed disorderly compared to the quasi-military explorers. None carried his helmet like any other; they marched out of step and clumsily; they let their environmental disorientation show.

"Only four!" Nali whispered hoarsely to a companion; "that's not a quorum!"

Himi spoke softly but with chilling authority: "Nali, this is to be an educational briefing, not a congress. We

24

shall informally explore the desirability of calling for a shipwide action, but that is the only decision called for by the circumstances at hand."

Even that, many thought silently, requires appropriate representation. But no one objected verbally; they were beginning to suspect that there was some unthinkable need for secrecy. Never before had a meeting in the nucleusphere been concerned not with unfolding a truth but with hiding one. As the meeting began and Himi let the withheld facts fall into place, the shocked participants exuded much oil and used a great many alcohol towels.

When the briefing was complete, Himi asked what seemed a peculiar question and directed it solely to the old scientist, Maoi:

"Is there anyone you now wish to include in this meeting?"

Maoi thought about it for what seemed an inordinately long time, looking into Himi's eyes, and finally replied: "No."

"I strenuously object!" Fera exclaimed, rising.

"To what?" Himi asked with a trace of sarcasm.

Fera did not answer because he suddenly understood what Himi had accomplished. With no quorum among the scientists, that group could not legally participate in a shipwide motion. There was no way to vote on whether or not to maintain secrecy, so secrecy was maintained by non-vote! And, although Himi had pronounced the briefing adjourned, no real adjournment was possible until the unaskable question was answered. The sixteen explorers and four scientists were stranded, sequestered like a deadlocked jury, until the scientists collected sufficient representation—or a message from the errant ship arrived—or the time extension expired. In spite of his on-going feeling of ill will toward Himi, Fera felt a sneaking admiration for the cleverness of Himi's political engineering.

Himi, standing away from the table, listened with interest and a smile; he caught phrases that arose from the whispered murmur: "...how much longer?...we under arrest?...not legal or ethical...guess he knew the others would let Maoi speak for them...call in the engineers, the food processors, then surely the whole ship would...willing to take that responsibility? I'm not...might even constitute treason...." Continuing to speak thus among themselves, the delegates from the outersphere made their way with downcast eyes back to the stairwell.

Nucleusphere attendants were deferential in the extreme toward their unexpected guests—offering them the best foods, the most comfortable beds, diversions from the executive library, even sexual gadgets to promote autogratification while they were kept from their wives. Some of the visitors enjoyed the unaccustomed luxuries; others seemed not to notice them at all. They waited.

Himi slept fitfully, often slumped over his instrument console.

When it finally came, Reno frightened everyone on duty by screaming inarticulately, "It's the signal!" He slammed his fist down on his console to close the switch that sounded an alarm in the guest quarters, summoning the explorers and scientists.

By the time Reno had tuned the signal and transferred its picture to the masterscope screen in the north hub of the sphere, Himi's breathing had slowed, and he clasped his hands together so tightly they began to hurt. He was only dimly aware that the others had taken seats at the conference table; he might have been alone in the

26

nucleusphere—or alone in the universe. For Himi, this was the worst moment; nothing that followed shocked him more than the sight of the pain, exhaustion, and resignation evident on his brother's face. "Hald . . ." Himi whispered his brother's name; already he suspected there would be no chance to tell him love and farewell. Himi's mind drifted momentarily into oblivion, but no one noticed.

"Himi, all my friends . . ." Hald began, forgoing any pretense at protocol. "As you can see, we still exist. But you are about to learn of so serious a tragedy that you must try to prepare yourselves. It will be worse than anything you might have been imagining. Reno, my dear friend, I assume you are as always manning the communications post; I suggest you first collect the compressed personal messages—written by many of us not so long ago really, but in happier times. We'll begin with the pen-pal notes for the children—"

Hald suddenly covered his face with his hands, and the screen faded to black. For a while there was only the buzz of the fast-speed recorded transmission that included no image. During the interval, Himi phoned down for a limitless supply of towels and for all attendants to stand by. The sinking feeling that chilled Himi's body was tempered somewhat by a new admiration for his brother: to be so self-possesed that he was able to cry while fully conscious!

"There is only one way I can get through all of this," Hald said when his telecast continued. "Himi, I will speak as if only you are hearing me. No, don't clear the nucleusphere," he said, a grim flicker of a smile passing over his lips, "I expect to be overheard. I think the gentlest procedure here is for me to begin at the beginning and tell the story as we experienced it. Let me remind you that although you heard from us only a little more than three years ago, that message was transmitted by us nine years ago. In the game of tag we play with time, dear big brother, I am now a few days older than you.

"Those nine years have surely included our best. We landed upon a verdant world at 24-245-6 that would be splendid for colonization. I have said so in my last report home. There were great oceans, thick forests, compatible animal life, and no sentient race to claim prior ownership. In many ways, the world was more beautiful than our home. For three years after we left the new planet, our people were busy night and day mapping, classifying, analyzing. Himi, I have never seen so happy and fulfilled a society.

"We traveled from there to binary 23-746-57, where we found two separate planetary systems. While we were scouting them, Himi, we learned a new emotional malady: that much excitement gave dozens of us—me included—a rash." Hald laughed. The memories were giving him back his youth and energy.

"Neither star possessed gaseous planets, and the cooler primary had only airless cinders for satellites. But two of the planets of the class 7 star had oxygen atmospheres! We concentrated on the larger, the second from the primary, because it had more nearly the dimensions of our home planet. After confirming, from atmospheric samples we scooped up, that both plant and animal life probably existed there in abundance, we landed.

"We found a fabulous planet: humid, breezy, covered with wonderful plant life—tree-height ferns, colorful herbs, mosses of every hue, a flowering shrub that released red globes filled with a warm gas that floated them away for pollination . . . here, I'll show you." Hald adjusted the controls before him and produced a series of

28

still photographs, landscapes of the weird alien planet.

Himi realized—while waiting for the picture of his brother to return—that Hald seemed alone in his nucleusphere. It was Hald, not his communications officer, who was operating the transmission and data-storage controls. Himi wondered if his companions here had also noticed; it seemed doubtful: they were captivated by fantasy pictures of red bubbles flying over a rainbow-colored hillside, under a hazy blue sky.

Hald's voice came with the final picture. "But nothing moved, except with the winds. There were no animals—" the landscape was suddenly gone and Hald's face had returned"—even though the carbon dioxide in the air indicated that there should have been, and in abundance. We tried numerous landing sights of various characteristics. Still no animals. We double-checked our conclusion that there was little or no volcanic activity that might account for the atmospheric carbon dioxide.

"Wherever we explored, we noticed a gray substance stuck to many of the plants; an analysis showed it to be a really remarkable substance—very nearly pure protoplasm. The stuff exhaled carbon dioxide, so it was considered animal in nature; but the gas emitted could never in millenia account for the atmospheric proportions we found there.

"We decided to excavate. Our archeologists had been busy no more than half a day when they began to unearth bones. Animal bones. The deeper they dug, the wider the variety of animal species they found. After the digs had proceeded to . . . oh, not so great a depth, the layers of carcasses ended and we reached nitrogen-rich soil and then a coal deposit. Perhaps you can imagine how eerie all that felt. Remember when we were children, Himi, and decided to explore the great sewer that led to the sea; and down there in the dark we could hear scavengers all around us, and we did not know whether we faced a real danger or only an imagined one. That's what I felt again when I heard the reports of the excavations.

"We considered bacterial or viral infection, some horrible plague; but our scientists found nothing of the sort in the bones, the soil, the plants or the air. Something, however, had evidently eliminated all animal life in the vicinity of our diggings, and likely upon the whole face of the planet, in a fairly short space of time, not too many centuries ago.

"We left the planet hastily—at the wrong time and wrong orbital placement for us to meet you on schedule—and radioed a message home placing this planet off limits until we could analyze the samples we brought with us." Hald stopped and removed a towel from his lap; he slowly wiped his forehead.

Himi signaled the attendants; now, he felt, was the time for towels and stimulants all around.

Hald continued: "Ilio-no-Rool died about half a year out. We were on our way to refuel at 23-989-6 and to make our scheduled contact with you. The situation was so puzzling that an autopsy was performed. Ilio died of lung congestion. The substance they found in him was the same as that gray slime back on the planet. His wife died some weeks later of what seemed to be a tumor. But again, it was the protoplasm slime. Then her other husband, Rado. Also lung congestion.

"Of course all our research was by then centered upon the parasite, or whatever it was. Both Ilio and Rado had been explorers and had actually walked on the planet's surface, breathing the contaminated air. We sealed off their quarters and hoped we had contained the parasite.

30

The other explorers were examined, X-rayed, and found to be healthy.

"It was discovered that the gray substance is made up of countless utterly separate cells, cells so simple there is no way to kill them except by methods that kill anything living—strong acids, fire, extreme cold, poisonous air, things of that nature. One physician called it a sticky virus; his description was voted down, but it's an effective metaphor. The cells are harmless on their own—like molecules of air—but when enough of them have collided to form something particle-sized, they begin to retain most of their own offspring. They grow into clusters, reproducing geometrically, of course. And the larger the cluster the faster it grows. We never discovered a way to detect a problem with the stuff in early stages; by the time we could see any of it in an X-ray, it would be on the verge of doubling in size. It's too late then. Also, we never devised a method of surgery that could promise to remove it all. If one breathes it, one will suffocate; if one eats or drinks it, the blockage will be gastric, unless the particle is minute enough to be assimilated—in which case the tumor can erupt anywhere: heart, muscle tissue, the brain."

Hald shivered visibly. He had been talking rapidly, as if the words he uttered were as repugnant as his subject, and had to be got out of the way. He breathed deeply. He continued:

"I'm sorry our scientists had no opportunity to prepare a fuller report on their findings; what little technical data we have has been relayed to you with those fast-speed communications. It must suffice that we have placed the planet on absolute quarantine. Someday, when there is need and opportunity, our people must go back and

31

annihilate it. As far as we know, the only other place in the universe it exists is here aboard our ship.

"We are a seething biological bomb. The entire outersphere is immersed in that gray slime. They even found traces of it in the vacuum of the innersphere— dormant. When they took cells of it to the labs, it came to life. Exposed to the cold of interstellar space, however, it does perish. Apparently, the innersphere is just warm enough to keep it from crystalizing.

"Miraculously, or so it seems to me, the nucleusphere is uncontaminated, so far anyway. Of course none of us who live here in the ball within the ball left the ship during the landing, and there was no physical contact with people of the outersphere—due to our hasty departure and the fact that the parasite was discovered while we were still under acceleration, when no traveling from sphere to sphere is possible. Thereafter, contact was forbidden in an effort to keep the infection contained.

"Do you see our trouble, Himi? We can't get out."

Himi tore his eyes from the screen; he could not look at his brother's face, and saw no need to force himself to. The others, he noticed, continued to stare—shocked, appalled, fascinated. The women of his officers had come up on deck. Himi had not summoned them; they had just come. Each held baskets of towels and stood near one or both of their husbands. Oado rested one hand on Reno's shoulder, and with the other she bathed his brow. She caught Himi's worried glance and smiled at him. Himi's first impulse had been to order them off the deck in order to protect them from what they were sure to hear. On second thought, he saw that they were holding up better than some of his men.

When Hald continued, his words were softer, more intimate. "The pilot officers and their families are all that

32

remain alive. We're purposeless wanderers who must reverse all our instincts and stay away from habitable planets, avoid the company of our own kind, and hope that no one will ever try to enter this ship to rescue us. In a rather close vote, we have decided not to endure a future of such isolation. There are other good reasons for the action we are about to take: when we die or the ship falls into hopeless disrepair, we might crash someday on some wonderful world; or worse, our computers might be able to take control and simply land us the first chance it gets; or someday, a passing vessel will discover our silent hulk and send their curious explorers to board us.

"You will be able to see our detonation. So, in fact, will the inhabitants of the third planet. To them, we will be an impossibility—a nova where there was never a star. We let our computers fulfill our original course instruction; we have made our passes through the fifth planet's atmosphere and now carry a full load of compressed fuel. We have programmed our thrust reactors to reverse their function and ignite the fuel that fills the shell around us." Hald seemed, like some mechanical man, to have run down. He froze as he was, as if he could not go on, or chose not to go on, or had said all there was to say, done all there was to do, and was now empty or dead. Himi glanced reflexively at Reno; he was slumped over his console, his hand dangling lifelessly over the edge of it. But his machinery was functioning without him— receiving, keeping the signal tuned, recording. Others, Himi noted, were out or drowsy; two were sprawled on the floor. About half of those present still kept their eyes hypnotically fixed on the blank-expressioned face on the giant screen.

"You must hear it all," Hald said sluggishly. "Himi, remember how we once declared that no mortal would ever understand how another could commit suicide, because the thought should render one too unconscious ever to accomplish the deed. That's not true. I can tell you the answer. We can kill ourselves when in terms of the future we are already dead.

"Carrying out our last communal directive, we have taken a painless poison. We voted to join our people, our graveyard in the outersphere, for our last moments, for a final act of sentimentality and affection—directed, I suspect, more at our ship and our mission than anything else. Our timing mechanism has been engaged. Our women and children wait for us now."

"I've told you so much because it's essential that you have no lingering questions. I know some part of you wants to be here with me, even now. Because of you, my dear brother, I have felt so powerful . . . like a man in two places at the same time . . . and all of creation belongs to us. Himi," he added, his face registering grim humor, "Just a few weeks ago, Jeno emerged. I have a son." Hald seemed annoyed that such a momentous revelation could be so insignificant. As if absent-mindedly, Hald lifted a paper from the shelf of the console; it held only a few words, but he seemed intent upon studying it for a long time.

"I assume you made the course correction that allows you to receive this message. It seems likely to us that your chronometer now reads—" he typed a question into the console keyboard and read the answer "—17:64:05, mark. Adjust for any amount I am off, and you will see our . . . our farewell at 18:06:76. You will not have time to respond to us, and that, I think you'll agree, is best."

Hald's eyes grew more energetic, his voice more purposeful. "I have work to do now. This communication

34

is ended." The screen went blank as Hald abruptly signed off.

Himi let his eyes rove from the screen to his shipmates. Three of them were still conscious. They returned his gaze—Oado, his wife; Fera, his antagonist; and old Maoi.

Chapter 4

The Hunters

Oado soothed her husbands as she would have her children—the more afflicted Reno first, then Himi, whose treatment was a smile of sympathy and admiration.

"You should be running this ship," Himi whispered to her as she cooled his face and hands.

Maoi got restlessly to his feet, apparently annoyed at the youthful instability of those groaning to consciousness around him. "It was overconfidence," he grumbled to Himi.

"Whose?" Himi asked listlessly.

"The impractical bastards who voted this gyroscopic design for the two ships—concentric spheres inside a spherical shell. Dangerous, impractical, inexcusable!"

Himi was not in a mood to debate the point. Perhaps later.

One self-possessed attendant, just arrived from below and intelligent enough to keep himself in total ignorance of the situation, distributed towels; another made stimulants available to any who wanted to accelerate a return to full awareness. Himi declined the artificial device.

Fera declined it indignantly, waving the extended hand aside.

Once again they felt themselves manipulated by a clock; this time the puppeteer was perverse, holding them only for the sake of holding them. This time they waited only for the end of waiting. The adjusted chronometer had to reach 18:06:76, and they had to see a nova where there was never a star. The screen was black and tranquil; the lighted numerals proclaimed 17:72:97 . . . 17:72:98 . . . 17:72:99 . . . 17:73:00 . . . 17:73:01. . . .

Oado assisted the attendants. She offered Fera a towel. He accepted it, but not gratefully. She was not offended, but she reflected, as she had many times, that her life had been saved on the day it was decided she would not marry Fera. Himi had been eloquent in directing the vote against Fera and in favor of Reno—simple, honest, sensitive Reno.

Oado, passing the time by studying Fera, thought idly: What would we be like if we were not taught levelheadedness as such a virtue? What if it is not emotion but rather a fear of emotion that so overwhelms people? Could it be that only those who never aspire to levelheadedness achieve it? Fera was the flaw in her theory. She felt certain that he had aspired to nothing more and nothing else—and he had achieved it profoundly.

She had once thought that allowing herself to make a fainting idiot of herself in young adulthood had "gotten it out of her system." But no, she reasoned now, it's that I was not afraid of feeling. I felt freely and learned my limitations. And ended up level-headed. Himi has surely done that too. But not Fera, who must have learned some

37

different and hidden method. It's as if Fera matured in some other universe, governed by other social and natural laws.

Thus engaged in philosophizing, an activity that would have surprised all but Himi, she observed the gradual revival of the officers, guests, women and attendants, and made note of their obsession with the clock—as if they waited almost eagerly for the new shock that was coming, the new test of level-headedness that this time they might pass. The numerals flashed 17:99:98 . . . 17:99:99 . . . 18:00:00 . . . 18:00:01, and the eyes stared, and the mouths were dumbly parted.

"Is there no one here alert enough to take action?" Fera asked without anger, plainly needling Himi more than anything else. "Significant fuel economies would result if we abruptly put ourselves back on course rather than waiting—"

"You're on your feet, Fera," Himi said, unruffled. "Go to the board and type in the instruction to return us to our prescribed course. We'll activate that instruction—when it's over. They . . . they believe we are waiting out the time with them. We owe it to them to really do so."

"Your sentimentality is expensive, Himi," Fera said softly as he strolled to the computer board and carelessly typed in the instruction. His manner told all that the task was so simple for him he could do it in his sleep.

18:03:22 . . . 18:03:23 . . . 18:03:24. . . .

Oado wondered if there might be some way she could persuade or trick Himi into taking a stimulant. She did not want him to show emotion or weakness with Fera here to gloat over it. When the moment came, Fera, she assumed, would weather it passively. She worried about Himi.

38

18:05:00 . . . 18:05:01 . . . 18:05:02. . . .

Mino, one of the explorers, suddenly jumped to his feet. "I know how to save them!"

That got their eyes off the clock, but they regarded him skeptically.

"It would take time, years, but if they could bore a narrow tunnel out through the axle of the nucleusphere, through the solid metal never exposing themselves to the innersphere even in pressure suits—"

A woman cried, "But there's no way to tell them—no time for a message to reach them!"

Himi raised his hand for silence. "The axle functions mainly as a support for cables; it extends out to a wheel that tracks around the equator of the outersphere. There is no direct solid-metal connection with the outside shell— not even the axle of the outersphere; it leads to a universal coupling. Don't think, my friends. Trust that they have considered everything. I trust that they have."

Fera reminded them: "Their vote to destroy themselves was not unanimous."

During the short time remaining, no word was uttered, no diversion attempted. Eyes oscillated between the ever-changing numerals of the clock and the masterscope that held the bright 23-989-6 surrounded by a now-familiar configuration of stars.

18:06:75 . . . *18:06:76* . . . 18:06:77. . . .

The time had passed; there was no explosion.

Several lost consciousness anyway; most stared, their eyes frosting over from dryness, until the clock read 18:08:00—when Fera spoke a single chilling word:

"Mutiny."

Reno rose angrily; Fera might have hurt him less with a physical blow. "No!" Reno protested the insult to his

39

people and to his co-husband's brother. He was too angry to formulate more of a retaliation. His whole benevolent concept of human nature had been attacked.

"Some mechanical difficulty," Himi said firmly, "or perhaps we have failed to allow time for the reaction to build—"

"Are you so naive that you cannot *imagine* anti-social behavior? Can you be certain that if your life had just been voted away you would meekly acquiesce? Their vote for self-destruction was *not unanimous!*" Fera growled.

"I think it must have been mutiny," said explorer Nali, with both grim resignation and a warmth directed toward Fera.

Urged on by the unexpected moral support, Fera continued extemporaneously building his case: "Hald said we would see the detonation. Are you people suggesting that his engineers and computers were unable to determine the simple line of sight—or that, after predicting our chronometer reading almost to the second, his time equation failed him?"

Fera continued his harangue, growing more and more confident as he constructed his case. Oado was observing keenly, tabulating the alarming support Fera commanded with so many explorers willing to follow Nali's lead. Ordinarily, she knew, Himi would have put a stop to Fera's nonsense; but now he had to tred lightly, try to seem more generous to Fera than Fera was to him. Oado did the only thing she felt empowered to do: as she wiped Himi's face, she slipped a stimulant into his mouth. He accepted it gratefully.

"They called for quarantine and annihilation of the contaminated planet," Fera spat out; "think how much more threatening that *ship* is! It is mobile, moving unpredictably from world to world. It might even attempt to return to our own planet! If mutiny has occurred, we must assume that the mutineers are either ignorant of the facts or simply don't wish to believe them. Or . . ." Fera paused before voicing yet another motive that occurred to him: "Or that in their bitterness, they would like to destroy all living things; if they are to die so senselessly, who could have the right to live?"

"No," Himi said flatly, interrupting Fera. "That is a motive of criminals. Whatever might turn out to be the truth here, that motive is one I will not even entertain."

"Nor I," said Reno; "and I propose we settle this at once. Have they criminal motivation?"

Nali asked Himi respectfully, "Under these extraordinary circumstances, may we not all vote? I think the outersphere deserves more than ordinary consideration today."

Himi was surprised—at Nali for being so bold as to request it, at the other explorers who did not disguise a glance at Fera to see his reaction, at Fera for so openly showing Nali and the others his pleasure, and at himself for realizing that he had no choice but to seek the favor of all of them by complying. "Yes, everyone here may vote on these matters," he said, hoping he sounded grateful to Nali for suggesting an obvious course.

The vote was a generous no—Hald's people were not guilty of criminal motivation. It was a victory for Himi; Fera's contingent granted it freely.

"Was it mutiny from some other motive, such as ignorance and self-preservation?" Fera persisted.

The vote showed that it was not, but the verdict was by a narrow margin.

"Are they dead?" Himi posed. "Either from the

41

contaminant or from poison? In other words, are we dealing with an inanimate virulent sphere—and a bomb that simply failed to function properly?"

By an even narrower margin than before, the group opinion was affirmative.

"Then," Himi quickly resumed, "we are dealing with an undirected vessel—derelict, dead—which must drift into perpetual orbit about 23-989-6. Are we in agreement?"

The vote was exactly tied. Himi employed his commanders' second vote to break the tie in his favor.

"Fera," Himi began firmly but courteously, "would you please go to the board now and activate the return to course you typed in earlier?"

Fera stood proudly, regal in his attitude of magnanimity, and took a few steps —knowing every eye was on his back—toward the control board. He stopped, turned, and suggested: "We are only a matter of months away from the fifth planet now. I submit that it would be wise to go there and refill the tanks we've emptied with all these course alterations. While there, we might conduct a search of the vicinity; if we locate the . . . biological bomb, we could push it into an orbit that would take it into the furnace of 23-989-6."

Reno noticed that Himi made no move to counter the idea. "It sort of makes sense," Reno muttered to him. Reno could see that Himi was stunned by the notion of serving as executioner of his brother's ship; he hoped no one else could see it. Particularly Fera. Reno turned to see if he could read Fera's mind in his eyes, but it was something behind the man that caught Reno's attention.

"Look!" Reno cried out jumping to his feet. One of the scopes at his station was alive with a regularly undulating composite wave form. "It's their distress beacon!" He announced it in amazement, not thinking efficiently enough to wonder about implications.

"Mutiny," Nali growled, clearly assuming that his high-placed friend had been vindicated.

Fera said, as if regrettably having to state the obvious, "Seek out and destroy them."

Those who next turned to Himi to see his reaction and seek his guidance found him slumped over the table unconscious. Oado had fallen to her knees behind his chair and was moaning pitifully.

Himi's weakness surprised many. Hadn't most of them been able to withstand this new shock? Even Reno, though dizzy, still held his eyes open; and Oado, a woman, still functioned. The guardian computer control had not even been activated.

"We must act now," said Nali, "while their beacon can still be traced. We must put Fera in charge."

Maoi rose; "Nali, these are not things for visitors to decide. It is an nucleusphere matter." He displayed indignation at Nali's impropriety, but it was also clear that he objected to Nali's proposal itself.

"We are all free citizens, old man," Nali responded. "Besides, Himi established that in this emergency we visitors might have a voting voice."

Oado wanted to speak. She wanted to say that yes, the situation on the other ship might indeed be mutiny; for now Oado could see how such a disgraceful thing might occur among otherwise honorable men—because she was seeing it happen, at this moment, on her own ship, to her own husband, by democratic vote, in the name of expediency in the face of an emergency. She said nothing. To these men, she knew, truth might come from a woman's eyes but never from her mouth.

43

The determination was not unanimous, but Fera was elected to assume command. Himi, when he awoke, would find himself the society's first past-President, now in the powerless position of consultant to the new regime.

For Oado, more than her government had fallen. Weakened to her limit, she gripped the back of her husband's chair for support while her mind flickered on and off.

Fera began shouting orders immediately, as if he had long rehearsed for this unforseeable event. "Get me the trajectory of the beacon's source...plot an intercept...ready the atmosphere scoops for re-fueling...Reno, radio the traitors; convince them we intend to effect a rescue...I don't care if they fail to acknowledge; they're listening...alert the outersphere to prepare for course-change acceleration...arm all explosive projectiles...."

Oado stared at Fera while technicians shouted their data back to him. She observed his satisfaction with his new situation. So now, she thought, they are being carried along by Fera as if he were safeguarding their very perception of truth. But have any of them any real perception of truth— beyond knowing where their vaga-bond faith currently lies? Does Fera himself know—or is he merely persuaded by their faith in him that he must be right? And round and round? Could this be what Fera has been after all along? Is this what power means to him? Only this? Is this the difference between Fera and Himi?

Those technicians concerned with sensing the universe outside their traveling world were working in concert to produce a telescopic view of the area of space occupied by the ship in distress. The masterscope flashed and wavered and broke up now into lines, now into dots, now resolving into a coherent picture, now shattering into components again. Oado's attention was drawn to it—pointlessly, she thought—perhaps because the mechanism of it was more intelligible to her than Fera's mind.

"There is still no answer from them, Fera," said Reno.

"We're getting our closest image," announced a masterscope technician.

On the great scope, against the familiar field of black, there appeared the crescent of a giant gaseous planet. This was their first look at the famous planet of fuel in this planetary neighborhood: mammoth by all measurements, streaked by violent winds, with a single red eye of turbulence now tangent to the terminator; it seemed to be an eye caught in the process of a wink.

It was gradual; it took most of them some time to realize what they were seeing and even longer to realize what it meant: a point of light lengthened into a line and this to a smear extending out from the night limb of the planet.

"They're burning propellant!" Reno gasped.

It was a sight none of them had seen before. Massive magnetic influences, solar winds, reactive molecules of outer atmosphere and other factors were combining to illuminate the ship's storm of propellant. In its desperate flight, the ship was fabricating the image of a comet.

"Now where are they going?" Fera demanded impatiently. "Give me their velocity, their orbit. Can we intercept?"

"They continue to accelerate."

"Propellant burn is over; they're in free fall."

"If they make further course corrections, they could orbit the third planet."

"Perhaps they intend to land there, to seek assistance."

"They still do not answer our call."

"Fera! They have discontinued their beacon! We have lost them!"

"But we know their trajectory..."

"If we follow them..."

"We can fill our tanks; we'll need capacity if..."

Himi, Oado saw, was awake, observing. He did not need to be told what was transpiring or what he had lost.

"Until we learn otherwise," Fera said with authority, "we must assume they will land and try to escape from their contaminated vessel. Are we in agreement there?"

The majority vote, Oado mused cynically, miraculously turned Fera's guess into a fact.

"If we cannot stop them before they land, we must be prepared to destroy the planet's ionosphere, render it uninhabitable. The planet possesses space travel and might spread the contamination farther if we allow it. Are we agreed on this point?"

The majority vote indicated to Oado that many of those present, particularly the explorers, ached for an exciting project and this suited the definition. But it established a death warrant for the third planet as firmly as would have a court of law.

Himi spoke calmly. "I, as an ordinary citizen of the nucleusphere, ask for a plebiscite on the decision to seek out and destroy. Are the risks, expenses, and potential gains reasonable?"

Oado felt no hope at all. It was merely Himi's only, and last, course of action.

The majority answer, almost a unanimous one, was proud and purposeful and altruistic:

Yes, seek out and destroy.

Part II

LOOKING OUT

Chapter 5

The Black Blot

"There's something going on we don't know about," a cub reporter from the Houston Explorer ventured to an ace from RBC-TV. They were at a crowded corner of the open bar at the rear of the NASA auditorium.

"Always is," muttered RBC, the ice in his plastic glass rattling as he took a long swallow. "Usually a surprise party for a returning astronaut or a crisis in plumbing somewhere."

The public address system came to life as a pleasant female: "May I have your attention? The NASA plex board is backed up with hundreds of calls waiting. May I ask that you keep your conversations short, and would those of you with sufficient power punch your calls directly through to the commercial boards in Clear Lake?"

RBC noticed Reuters replacing a phone in her purse. "What's up?" he asked her.

"Couple of things. So naturally my office had to call

me twice. Some radio scopes are picking up peculiar signals from Jupiter. I'm supposed to ask what they are. Second call—and this might yet get us a hard story out of this soiree—tells me a Washington copter was cleared to land here an hour ago, carrying guess who—"

"George Washington?"

"Daniel Copalin."

Global, NBC, and the New York Times were eavesdropping. They said in a comic chorus: "The Black Blot!"

At last RBC's own phone beeped. He lifted it from his shirt pocket, set it on "confidential" and extended the ear piece to shut out his competitor-comrades. "Yes?"

"You've heard about Copalin's arrival? They say he's going to confer his Black Blot on some NASA project. Set up with Petersen; he's got two cameras there on the floor somewhere. We can hit live in the middle of newscasts in eight time zones, so comb your hair."

"Is this important?"

"I doubt it. But the old Black Blot is news these days. Oh, and our spy tells us they've let Bud Sullivan jet over from Canaveral to make an appearance. He hasn't even been debriefed. His shuttle touched down just this morning."

"What's he been doing?"

"Gathering meteors in the spring, tra-la. Something to do with Delta Colony. Same old thing."

Practically any member of the working press could supply Bud Sullivan's vital statistics: born and raised mostly in Dallas, 31 years old, 1.85 meters, 76.2 kilograms, red-brown hair, green eyes. Sullivan's image was stuck onto boys' lockers at shoool; girls put him into a category with popular singers and TV stars; and adults looked to him for wisdom—after all he had been everywhere a man could possibly go, had lived longer on the moon than anyone in history. He always handled himself in front of the multimillions in his TV audiences with the utmost confidence, as if he spoke only to a handful of trusted friends. The public needed him. The press, contrariwise, generally thought him agreeable, dull, pretty, phoney, but worth his weight in air minutes and semicolons.

The NASA press secretary was introducing him:

"... longest mission since his stay on the moon two years ago when he assisted in the bringing on stream of the mass-driver that made the lunar mines fully operational. Now if I don't shut myself up, I'll start telling you about his latest mission," the secretary confessed, "because I am personally so excited about it. Bud Sullivan."

He entered looking even more striking than usual. He wore one of NASA's newest space garments and carried his bubble of a helmet. The new suits were practically skin tight, affording maximum maneuverability and requiring minimal pressurization. He did indeed look like a knight in silver and orange and blue.

"He forgot the cape," RBC muttered to the cub from the Houston Explorer.

At the podium, Bud smiled and said simply, "Hi. Let me just fill you in on what we've been doing out there."

The astronaut paused a shade too long. Celia Thompson—personalities editor for the Star Syndicate—had time to interject:

"Who did you come home to, Bud?"

The reporters all recognized the husky voice of the world-famous busybody. Many of them groaned quite audibly.

49

Celia risked losing a scoop by asking her question publicly, but this particular risk paid off: a split second before Bud broke into an amused grin, his eyes had darted, probably involuntarily, to a small attractive woman who was standing by the door through which Bud had entered the theater.

"No one you know, Celia," he quipped good-naturedly; then he deflected the subject. "Although there's been no time for editing, I have some pretty spectacular pictures to show you; please bear with the redundancies...." As he spoke, the theater's photogrid was being lowered from the ceiling.

The NASA grid was the world's largest. Union Photogrid Ltd. had presented it to NASA in recognition of the space agency's role in developing it—and as a public relations gimmick. This grid was made up of microscopic color clusters of liquid crystals sensitized in the manner of old-fashioned computer cores. The picture it showed looked like an enormous unilluminated moving photograph. Tube television was finally on its way out, many believed.

"...bricks were made at the zero-gravity plant—that thing there that looks like a molecule model—out of the slag from a metals-refining process. The purpose, as I think you know, was to add a layer around the exposed portions of the Delta cylinder...." The picture showed the view from a ship approaching the overwhelmingly vast and complex 10,000-inhabitant colony. This was the most finished the colony had looked in pictures either brought or transmitted back. The cylinder was finally closed; the solar collectors were in place; swarms of robot vessels tugged at cabling; tiny points of light were free-floating silver-clad men clustered here and there where work was in progress.

It was kind of interesting, Celia thought, but she had work to do. Her eyes had never left the girl—who had just slipped back outside the door. Celia exited through the rear by the bar and, being familiar with the outside corridors, set an intercept course.

On a long bench beside a high green-plastic door, the mystery-girl looked even smaller than she had inside. Perhaps all of a meter and a half tall, Celia guessed. Words were already forming in the typewriter of the gossip journalist's mind: pretty and peppy and frail. Business-like short black hair. Big dark eyes.

The victim looked up. "Hello, Ms. Thompson," she said—without much enthusiasm, Celia thought.

"You have the advantage, Ms.—?"

"I think I'll hang onto that advantage," she said pleasantly.

"May I sit?" From Celia's past experience, a woman having an affair with a national hero was always dying to talk about it. "Tell me about you and Bud Sullivan," she challenged bluntly.

"Isn't it time to start leaving Bud alone?" the young woman asked sincerely. Then she shrugged and said, "But come to think of it, I suppose he enjoys the attention."

The girl had confirmed nothing, but she had missed her opportunity to deny it. "You are having an affair with him!" Celia declared triumphantly. "What's your name? I'll find out anyway, so why not save me the trouble?"

"How did you get Bud and what's-her-name to cavort naked on the beach for your TV cameras?" the girl asked, ignoring Celia's question.

"Off the record, what's-her-name helped me set it up. Bud loved the show, you know. He called me after the telecast and said he thought it had been done artistically and tastefully."

51

Unexpectedly, the girl laughed. "Listen, I don't resent you for the kind of work you do," she said, "but I really have nothing to tell you."

Celia thought: either this creature is crazy, or I am. This conversation can't be happening! At close range, Celia was beginning to think the girl's face looked vaguely familiar. "Do you work here at NASA?"

She nodded. "In image enhancement. I was on the crew that developed the photogrid technology."

"Thanks for the clue."

"In fact, I ought to be in there thinking about liquid crystals, molecular color, and contrast refinement. These are some of the best-photographed tapes we've ever had on the big screen. Care to join me? We can sneak in the back way—the way you must have snuck out."

Director Clark was at the podium. "If there are no more queries relating to Bud's report, we have two more items of business that I think you'll find newsworthy. Our plex board has been lit up like a Christmas tree during the last few hours. It seems that a great number of satellite receiving stations, long and short-wave radios, even commercial television in some areas, have been picking up mysterious signals from outer space. I've asked our Dr. Greitzer to tell you what we know about it."

Greitzer was such a stereotype of "the scientist" that there was a sudden flurry of camera activity as he stepped lazily onto the podium. He was gaunt, gray, bespectacled and sleepy looking.

When he began to speak the image faded somewhat; his voice was crisp and energetic. "An organized transmission of some kind has been received over approximately half of the globe, the hemisphere that would be affected if the transmission came from roughly the present position of the planet Jupiter. Visually displayed, the signal became a composite wave form that changed every 9.3 seconds. Thank you."

The scientist moved as if to leave the podium but was stopped by a roar of simultaneous questions from the floor. He waited for the gibberish to subside and then said, as if addressing a classroom, "One at a time, please. Yes—you there."

"Is there any content to the signals?"

"It seems unlikely, as there is no variety in information bits."

"Could the signal be naturally caused, or may we assume that there's an intelligence behind it?"

"I suggest you make no assumption at all."

"Might it be a man-made transmission?"

"Plain static can be man-made, young man."

"Well, might it be a natural phenomenon?"

"That would be odd, but it might."

"Let me get this straight. You are saying that the signals were probably sent by intelligent life from the vicinity of Jupiter?"

"What I am saying is that we just don't know."

Greitzer withstood the barrage of questions with an amused smile, as he might have faced a panel of colleagues after delivering a controversial research paper. At last a reporter managed to add a final bit of information by asking:

"Are the signals continuing, or have they stopped?"

"They have apparently stopped. They came in regularly spaced bursts and then ceased."

"Like a beacon flashing past?"

"Metaphorically."

53

The reporters lapsed into murmuring among themselves. Dr. Clark deftly replaced Greitzer on the podium and stood silently for a moment. He waited for the ladies and gentlemen of the press to begin to wonder what he had saved for last on the program. It worked. Soon most of them faced front expectantly. Clark's first words startled them:

"We are not afraid of Senator Daniel Copalin."
When the brief but distinct furor diminished, he continued: "Some of us here even admire his audacity and agree with some of his tactics. We believe, however, that he has overstepped his prerogatives this time, and we intend to answer his allegations. We invite him to the podium at once, so that today both sides of the controversy he will introduce can be presented. Senator Copalin."

The dignified 55-year-old Senator from New York received enthusiastic applause from the press as he ascended the speakers' platform.

"Thank you, Dr. Clark," he began, "for inviting me to address this gathering. Good afternoon, ladies and gentlemen of the press here at the Spacecraft Center, and those of you watching this telecast worldwide. I assume, perhaps egocentrically, that many of you are familiar with my current campaign to further reduce government expenditures in all areas not directly related to the protection of the rights of our citizenry; to reduce spending, to reduce taxes, to increase the individual economic freedoms in this land. My record has proved—I won't say impressive, I'll say fairly good. I have no legal powers, as you know. I merely point out instances of waste—dramatically. I am proud to announce, incidentally, that in this fiscal year alone more than 100 million dollars have been saved, or rather not spent, at

54

least in part as a result of my Black Blot campaign."

The Senator took a document from his breast pocket and unfolded it for the television cameras to see. It was a plain white sheet of letterhead stationery with a paragraph or so typed on it, and, at the lower right, the familiar irregularly shaped black ink blot. He read from it:

"Throughout the past number of decades, there have been various ill-advised and terrifically expensive attempts made to contact hypothetical alien races on profoundly distant stars. Some of these radio transmission and reception systems have been funded privately. But now there is the Starprobe Relay—an attempt to build a virtually unending fleet of robot ships to sail out into our galaxy. Starprobe is being underwritten by the United States government at astronomical—pun intended and emphasized—cost to the taxpayer. The Starprobe scientists concede that even should their experiments be successful, it might be years—even centuries—before results might show themselves. The project leaders contend that public funding is necessary because such billions would not be forthcoming voluntarily from the unsophisticated general public. I say that *that* is precisely why public funding must stop. If the public would not willingly support the project, then the use of public funds constitutes expropriation. I Senator Daniel Copalin, Democrat from the State of New York, and elected servant of the United States government, therefore confer upon the Starprobe Relay project the Black Blot, in the hope that this gesture will lead to a full and final discontinuance of the unjustifiable public venture."

There were voices raised, and hands shot into the air. Copalin blithely ignored them all and by grand gesture invited Dr. Clark back to the microphone.

Clark said: "I have asked the head of Starprobe to speak on behalf of the NASA staffs here." He looked toward a side door where a man stood waiting. "Dr. William Reid."

Only ten or twelve of the reporters gathered there at NASA had met William Reid, and only a handful more clearly remembered the brief announcement of his appointment to Starprobe two years ago. No sensational follow-up news stories had resulted from it. The man they watched approach and ascend the platform looked far too young to be in charge of a program significant enough to warrant Senator Copalin's attention. Reid was around thrity. He was thoroughly medium: medium height, build, weight, coloring and of average attractiveness. "He should have been a bank robber," CBS said to Reuters; "no one would ever have been able to identify him."

He was dressed casually in brown denims, a short-sleeved white pullover, and his tennis shoes were ancient and worn through in a number of places. It seemed safe to assume that he had been summoned hastily. When he faced the crowd their attitudes toward him changed: he now seemed like a man waiting, blindfolded, before a firing squad.

"I told Dr. Clark that I was the wrong man to speak in defense of Starprobe," Reid began, not bothering to address his audience formally, "because I am so closely involved that it is utterly beyond me that anyone at all could oppose it. All my life I have felt helpless in the face of having to explain the self-evident. I cannot answer the Senator's charges."

The reporters were oddly spellbound. Even when it

56

seemed that he had stopped, capitulated without a statement, they remained silent. Reid finally continued:

"It was never our intention, of course, to expropriate tax dollars for a venture that has insufficient support. It's just that federal funding seemed by far the most efficient means." Again it seemed that Reid had no more to say. His head was down, neither looking into the many television lenses nor at the reporters seated before him. "We have just begun to work on the hardware for the first of the probes," he resumed. "The planning has taken more than two years. Indirectly, it has been underway since the first flight of the Wright Brothers. No, since Columbus... since we left the caves. If funds are withdrawn now, it will be like...." He lifted his head and raised his voice slightly; his eyes glistened. "Like cutting off the head of humanity."

Science News turned to the Smithsonian Magazine and whispered: "Why doesn't he explain what the program *is*? I could defend it better than this!"

The woman from the Smithsonian shook her head as if to say: It beats me. Then she had an idea. She blatantly interrupted Reid before questions had been invited and asked—it sounded loud in the silence—"Do *you* believe it possible, Dr. Reid, that the Jovian signals we just heard about might be from an intelligent race, from extraterrestrials?"

Reid looked up, surprised; the tension in his face eased somewhat. "Not if the signals are coming from Jupiter. I tend strongly toward the ecosphere theory which holds that there is only one possible life chemistry, that it can develop only under specific conditions, and that those conditions obtain only at certain distances from a given sun. Jupiter is too far beyond our ecosphere to have evolved life systems. However—since you brought it up—I am encouraged in the belief that many many suns have planets, many of them within ecospheres. There could be many thousands of intelligent races out there; in fact, it seems almost a certainty."

National Geographic joined the other pro-Starprobe reporters by asking: "Would you agree that it's likely that the signals come from intelligent beings but from far out in interstellar space, coincidentally in line with the present position of Jupiter?"

Reid at last seemed at ease; he knew he was talking to friends. "Well, no. Something similar to this happened back in the 1970's. Americans were very excited by reports in Pravda that the Russian radio-telescopes had isolated a clear and strong alien signal. In the U.S., scientists had no luck corroborating their evidence, but they couldn't believe it was all a fabricated story. Why lie about a thing like that? To make this long story short, here's what turned out to be the truth. We had a satellite in an extremely high orbit that was designed to photograph Russian military installations through infra-red filters and other devices. On the satellite's regular pass over Pasadena, it was to dump the compressed and encoded information. You can guess what was happening. The transmissions were out of sync. Our robot spy was photographing the U.S. and dumping the pictures, encoded, over Russia. I'd want to eliminate that kind of thing before looking for more exotic possibilities."

"He threw it away!" Science News hissed. "He could have made it seem *mandatory* that we send Starprobe out to explore for alien civilizations."

Dr. Clark stepped to Reid's side. He said, "I've spoken to Dr. Vladimir Merzhkovsky in Moscow. They didn't know what I was talking about; they received no such signals."

"They're in the wrong hemisphere," Greitzer said, stepping forward.

It was difficult to tell whether his associates stepped up to give Reid moral support or to shut him up. The many quick questions that followed were merely attempts to pin down one scientist or another and get a prediction. Reid left the answering to Clark, Greitzer and Bud Sullivan.

Celia Thompson and her lady-in-question had been watching from the back. When it became evident that Clark was about to adjourn the meeting, the girl left Celia without a word and made her way—Celia was astounded to note—around the outside of the seated audience to where Senator Copalin was standing. Suddenly everyone was milling about, heading toward the bar; and Celia had to be downright rude to be able to force her way toward the Senator and the girl.

The girl lifted the Senator's hand to her mouth and bit it. He yanked his hand away and pulled her hair affectionately. Oh sweet Jesus! Celia howled internally; she's Gari Copalin—the Senator's daughter!

Celia continued the swimming motions that effectively got her through the knots of people. She followed Gari Copalin to the speakers' podium. Bud Sullivan was standing close to her but not touching—looking at her though. Gari slipped her arm through Dr. Reid's. She steered him toward the side door.

Celia's mouth dropped. She sat down and frowned.

The paging system was suddenly active again: "Dr. Greitzer, Dr. Hanson, Dr. Clark, Mr. Sullivan, Mr. Grant, Senator Copalin, you have calls waiting. . . ."

Chapter 6

A Jovian Comet

Why am I heading north? Dr. Reid asked himself out of idle curiosity. He was approaching Dallas. Just driving.

It was all over in Houston. They had offered him a staff job of some kind - right now he couldn't recall what. Senator Copalin's time bomb had exploded after only a seven-week fuse. Almost all of NASA's current projects had at least a remote connection with issues relating to defense; but, as Copalin had told the Congressional subcommittee: "We really are under no clear and present danger from the mythical beasts of Andromeda."

The prairie hills of Texas rolled by; dead grasses at the roadside bent back like water parting for a speedboat; the gray evening sky had closed over, as if maliciously to hide the sunset.

He kept hearing Senator Copalin's voice at the subcommittee hearing in Washington:

"If, as Dr. Reid claims, there is an idealistic will to know in the land, he must act on his conviction and get people to put their money where their ideals are—fund his dream privately!"

And maybe, William thought, after 20 years of fund-raising and cheap notoriety, like some sleazy Twentieth Century evangelist, I could pave the way for younger men to do my work for me.

He flicked on his car radio to quell the Senator's ideas and his own self-pitying ones. The splendid conclusion of a romantic symphony rushed into the plastiglass bubble as it whisked along. It was so contrary to William's mood that it was like a stifling blast of hot air. Before he could switch it off, it had awakened his companion.

"Sorry, Ganymede," Reid said when the volume was down. He had said it as if addressing a friend, a peer.

Ganymede yawned. She was curled around herself on the passenger seat, one paw under her head and the other lazily draped over the seat edge. Ganymede was small for a Weimaraner (a runt, to use a word William never would have), but otherwise she was perfect. Silver gray with an egg-shaped white smear on her chest, she had pale gray eyes that, when she was excited, opened all the way to show big black pupils. Her face seemed to frown at the world and smile in inward satisfaction at the same time. Master and dog looked a bit alike.

"Sledway 9 km," said the glowing diodes at roadside, and Reid suddenly had a reason for driving north. He followed the sign's direction and turned off onto a side road.

When he stopped under the lighted hyperbolic arch that marked the entrance to the Sledway, the toll clerk asked him, "How are you powered?"

"Internal combustion—hydrogen fuel."

"Really? In that little thing? Install it yourself?"

"Yes."

61

"We'll have to evacuate your water pan before putting you on the sled."

"Fine; it's easy to do."

"Equipped with a multichannel phone?"

"Yes"

"Need an auxiliary battery for the trip?"

"No, I have plenty of power—fuel cell."

"Can I rent you a TV. We're showing a choice of seven movies."

"I thought I'd just go as far as Oklahoma City. I don't think that's time enough for a movie, is it?"

"Nope. But why not go on through to Kansas City? You're just a sight-seer, right? I can see it on your face. Why not go all the way?"

"Well . . . what *are* the seven movies?"

All the way, Kansas city with TV, a frozen gourmet dinner and a microwave slot, a couple of martinis, chopped beef for Ganymede, and several of the latest magazines.

The sled that had been attached beneath Reid's wheels advanced the car without a wobble, without his giving it a command, and without a sound. Ganymede sat up and peered through the windshield as if she too were anticipating something. The car shot under another arch and out onto a deep-curving ribbon in the air. It was easy to imagine that the car had sprouted wings, but not even aircraft were this free of vibration and sound. The vehicle rode on barely an inch of air and was moved forward by a steady electromagnetic pull. The six northbound lanes of the Sledway appeared below like an airport runway. William felt a fierce regret that so few cars were on it. Somehow, he felt, this wonderfully futuristic venture just had to succeed. The access ribbon was no longer a curve; it descended to place William in the outermost lane. The speedometer the toll clerk had clipped to his window was at 165 kph and climbing. William laughed aloud as the Sledway's computers rearranged the existing traffic so he could enter their midst. It was like a precision routine performed by a marching band. For the first time in seven weeks, William—luxuriating in the experience of something promising and untried—was happy.

William could still see the glow of Dallas behind him, and his speedometer stood fixed at 396.7 kph—when the phone rang.

William flipped the two-way. "Yes?"

"Bill?"

"William."

"Yeah, it's you. This is Bud Sullivan."

"I remember Bud Sullivan, the rocket jockey."

"What's wrong? You sound happy."

"I'm having fun."

"Well drop it and get up to McDonald Observatory."

"McDonald isn't up anymore; it's down. I'm on the Sledway."

"For God's sake. Well get off it."

"I can't. It's the Sledway! What's going on?"

"Get an RBC station on your radio. They're still talking about it. They've sighted another burst at Jupiter. Or rather *we* have, here at McDonald. The press has dubbed it the putt-putt comet because it keeps reappearing. But of course it isn't a comet at all."

"What is it?"

"Little green men on Jupiter sending up flares, or maybe on one of Jupiter's moons—maybe Ganymede. Hey, is Gany with you?"

"Ganymede with me. You know there's nobody on Ganymede; we've landed probes there."

"We got a spectrograph this time. The streak is

63

radioactive water and free hydrogen."

"That's interesting, but—"

"Help us prove there's a little green man up there, and I'll show you how to get all the money you want!"

William was about to convert the sad shaking of his head into words when another voice addressed him:

"William, it's Gari. Try to dump everything this idiot has told you. Just turn on RBC, quickly, and then get to McDonald as fast as you can. I've read about the Sledway; they have a rather expensive emergency procedure that phases you over and off onto a shoulder. If you have to, get a copter to pick you up. This is more than interesting—whether it means little green men or not. Here, take down this call-back number: 915-5927-0038-2. But don't use it. We'll wait for you here. Bye."

As he tuned in RBC, William wondered how on earth Bud Sullivan managed to tie up with someone who could be so succinct.

Through numerous periods of rejuvenation, the 2.7-meter reflector at McDonald Observatory, in the Davis Mountains of West Texas, had remained in constant use since its completion in 1969. Its use at this time was almost exclusively that of training tool for student astronomers from Universities in Texas, New Mexico, Oklahoma and Illinois. It was an unexpected place, William Reid felt, for any sort of exclusive discovery. Yet the RBC newscaster had given McDonald sole credit for the recent sighting.

The sky was clear, the moon was bright, and Reid— flying over Toyahvale Pass in his rented copter—could pick out the stark canyon wall and pinon pine grove to which the four of them— Bud, Gari, Ganymede and himself—had once hiked and picnicked. Ahead was Mt.

Locke, a mile-high jumble of boulders, cliffs, giant oaks, pine and juniper, patches of bald earth and patches of cactus; and crowning it the chalky-white observatory domes. The main structure was a venerable antique that gave one simultaneously the impressions that it was eternal and obsolete.

Reid began to see over the top of Locke into the valley beyond where the far edge of the Harvard-Hillary 400-meter radio telescope was sliding into view. Like some crazily symmetrical web woven by an unthinkably huge robot spider, the radio dish looked anything but obsolete—but it was. The dish had suffered the same fate as Starprobe: federal and state funds had been withdrawn midstream and it had been eight years before a $30 million private endowment, from a Mr. Leon T. Hillary, had started crews working again. During that time, a federal "defense-oriented" dish far outclassing the Harvard-Hillary had been erected on the east limb of the moon, at Marginis. Harvard-Hillary now served mostly as a backup and relay for its lunar superior, and not much more. It too seemed an unlikely participant in the discovery RBC-radio had ascribed to it.

Reid easily spotted Bud's black-and-orange copter down below in the lot adjoining the sprawling three-story cliffside structure where the 60-odd scientists, teachers and students lived and worked. It was two o'clock in the morning, but all the lights of the building were on and projecting yellow trapezoids on the lightly frosted ground.

"Hold onto your stomach, Ganymede."

A longer bright trapezoid fanned out on the parking lot; Reid watched his welcoming party cast their long shadows through it out toward his landing target. They stopped at a safe distance, their windbreakers flapping in the copter's downdraft. He recognized Bud, Gari, and Dr. Dubin, a director of the telescope and an acquaintance of several years; the identity of the fourth was revealed to him as they escorted him across the lot:

"Billy Boy," Bud intoned jovially, "meet Mr. Leon T. Hillary. Leon, meet NASA's most starry-eyed idealist, Dr. William Reid. . . ."

Hillary was a tall overweight man wrapped in buckled-down leather. His hand-tooled boots and Texas wide-brim tried hard to proclaim him a cowboy. He shook Reid's hand firmly and said not a word.

Ganymede was last through the door. She yawned, stretched her hind legs and ambled in.

"Just before sunset tonight," Dr. Dubin began, trying to be systematic in his presentation to William Reid, "the Hillary radio picked up a burst of energy, very noisy energy, from close in, about 551,000 kilometers from Jupiter, suggesting an orbit—"

"But it's not a comet," Bud interjected impatiently.

"We trained our 2.7 reflector on—" interrupted a lanky technician Reid knew to be David Trombatore, a normally quiet, competent recluse who had found his home on isolated academic Mt. Locke.

Gari restored order by cutting in to ask, "What did you do with your car?"

Reid laughed. "By now it should be at the copter rental place in Dallas."

They were in the conference room of the McDonald installation, where the tables were strewn with instruments, video playback units, computer print-outs, and spectrograph plates.

Dr. Dubin resumed, unchallenged this time; "We alerted both orbiting observatories and other ground-based telescopes, but we got the drop on all of them and surely have the best data. By the time they could set up to verify our findings, the phenomenon was dissipating. As I said, the image was very noisy, so we ran a computer enhancement and came up with this." He pointed out the transparency before William on the table. It looked very much like the picture of space an optical telescope might yield, not the conventional linear graph of a radio telescope. The computer had transformed the signal into a visual counterpart.

"I don't think I'd call that a comet, either," William said. He compared the picture against numerical data on the print-outs. "First I'd suspect, oh, a collision of debris with a minor moon, exploded matter from the Jovian atmosphere, an old atomic-powered earth probe breaking up. Tell me, I'm curious, how did you happen to be right on the spot to observe this?"

Gari muttered, "They had nothing better to do."

"I suppose there's truth in that," Dubin agreed. "But it was largely Mr. Hillary here who kept us on our toes. He took such a keen interest in that first sighting and radio disturbance that he's had us searching for others."

William frowned, said, "Oh," and indicated Dubin should continue telling the sequence of events.

Leon Hillary—his hat removed, displaying a bush of gray hair that reminded William he'd seen pictures of Hillary before——leaned against the wall and was contributing nothing to the briefing. He stared at William Reid, though, as if attempting to influence him through ESP.

William interrupted Dubin's continuing narrative to ask, "What wave lengths registered the image?"

"It was noisiest at 21 megahertz," David Trombatore answered.

"Hydrogen," William said, nodding. "What did you

67

get on other bands? Anything that looked like encoded transmissions, as you'd get from an unmanned probe?"

Hillary stirred; he said in his deep growling drawl, "They would contact us on 21 megahertz."

"Who?" Reid asked, afraid he knew the answer.

"The aliens. They'd know we'd be listening to 21, because that's the most fundamental frequency of the universe. You can bet on it."

Reid turned, not hiding his doubt very politely, and said to Dubin, "I suggest you do a full scan of the logical broadcast range—soon, before we lose line of sight with Jupiter. And contact the orbiting observatories to continue the search, in every band other than 21—which is just noise."

Dubin lifted a phone from his shirt pocket and punched up a number.

"Why bother?" Hillary asked, apparently not offended.

Reid answered, thinking it out as he went along, "Assume that it *is* aliens. Assume, in fact, that this is not the same shipload of them that caused the disturbance seven weeks ago. Assume it's a fleet of aliens. If it is, then why assume their aim is to contact *us*? Perhaps we'll be able to overhear them just talking among themselves. Besides, if it is an old exploratory probe from earth, and there's anything left of it, it might be returning a code we can recognize, one that would allow us to identify it."

Hillary shook his head. "They would not be here except to contact us."

When he finished his telephone calls, Dubin picked up where he had left off. "Some of what you wanted has already been done. Results will be sent to us shortly. We did a spectrographic analysis that indicates very energetic radiation; we'll have that data compiled in a half hour or

68

so. I've set up a conference call with observers in orbit and the staffs at Marginis, Palomar and Deer Creek—to take place at four o'clock. Would you like some coffee?"

Reid smiled. "Two cups—at least."

"You blew it, William."

"Hillary? He's the reason you wanted me here, isn't he?"

"Yep."

Bud, William and Gari leaned against the cold metal of William's rented copter. The breeze was chilly and as steady as a fan exhaust. Horizontal shafts of pink light had brought dawn to the top of distant Mt. Livermore and soon would touch the pines that rimmed the parking lot at McDonald.

"If you'd gone along with Tex's alien-mania, you'd have ended up on his payroll," Bud persisted.

"Like Dr. Dubin?"

"Like Dr. Dubin."

"Tell me about Hillary. Who is he?"

"Leon T. Hillary," Bud said, in the manner of a newscaster, "bought at auction, about 20 years ago, a parcel of land the government had once set aside for a park. He got it for a song—right place at the right time—and set up the Limpia Canyon Ranch. Amusement park, dude ranch, gambling casino, retreat for the weary, you name it. He raked in enough to allow him to bid on Big Bend, and got a prime chunk of it. Of course land use was restricted to recreational stuff, but that's just what he wanted it for. He's the one who installed the cable cars, observation balloons, rustic hotels, more casinos—at a time when practically everyone had seen all they wanted to of Grand Canyon. Right place at the right time again. Know what he's been pouring his profits into? Crackpot religious

69

organizations—mostly one that claims Jesus was an alien do-gooder who's due to come back and explain what he meant to say the first time around. And you just told the man his messiah is an atomic rattletrap from before the turn of the century which last night splattered itself all over the solar system."

"You see," said Gari, "why he wanted to buy himself an observatory."

"Oh, come on. Gari, he didn't—" Bud insisted.

"Yes he did," she said with a shrug.

"I don't want my name associated with Hillary's—in any way at all," William said coolly.

"That's suicidal! He couldn't single-handedly finance your Starprobe, but if he got all his addlebrained million-aire friends together I bet he could!"

"And I'd have to design the transmissions around 21 megahertz and send the Relay ships toward the star where they think their God lives. I'd be a tool of religious fanatics." William added: "Like Dr. Dubin."

"Are you saying this Jupiter thing should have been left undiscovered? What if Hillary is right?"

"Hillary can't be right. Even if everything turns out just as he predicts, I'll see it as just a silly coincidence. Hillary *knows* nothing."

"Why did you come here?"

"Oh, I was curious— but mainly because you and Gari asked me to."

Gari shivered. She leaned against Bud, who wrapped his arms around her shoulders. "What were you holding back in there?" she asked William. "You didn't tell Dubin and Hillary all you were thinking; I could see it on your face."

William snorted. "I wasn't sure I wanted to tell Bud, either."

"Tell," Bud demanded.

"The puzzler is that there were *two* comet-like objects. How likely could it be that two old atomic probes blew up only seven weeks apart after decades of inactivity?"

"My God!" Bud said, "you do think it's aliens!"

"It doesn't seem impossible. But my main objections still stand. Alien visitations just aren't practical; you don't go roaming around the galaxy dropping in on inhabited planets. That consumes many generations of travelers, too much expense, with too little promise of results. Maybe there are civilizations out there capable of it; but it would be as crazy for them to do it as for us."

Bud smiled. "What if Hillary rounded up all his true believers and proposed taking off with them for Alpha Centauri. Bet he could do it. Maybe our visitors at Jupiter are cosmic evangelists, little green Hillaries out to find *their* God?"

"What a grizzly thought," said Gari. "I think I have a better hypothesis for you. What if there are two alien unmanned probes—their version of a Starprobe Relay?"

Ganymede had been exploring the pines and junipers. She trotted up to the group and, ignoring them in a trustful way, jumped through the open door into the warmer copter. William reached in and rubbed her back, leaving his elbow resting on her rump. "I hope," he said to his friends, "you won't spread these notions around until I've had time to do more checking. I'm waiting for Dubin to run me off copies of all the data."

Bud rapped on his friend's skull. "Always churning. Let me see if I can hurry Dubin along. Here, William, keep the midget warm till I get back." Unexpectedly, he guided Gari into William's arms and placed her head against his chest.

They watched Bud run, like the college track star he

71

once had been, across the lot. He pulled open the door and disappeared inside.

William thought that he should release Gari, but his arms paid no attention to his mind. He found that he was irritated by the screeching of birds, the hissing of pine needles; and the dawn seemed too bright: the top of the main McDonald dome was burning with a peach incandescence.

"Is he flaunting his trust of us?" William wondered aloud, softly.

"I guess he wants us to go ahead and get it over with," she said.

William removed his arms from her shoulders.

"I'm still cold," she said. William could not see her face; but the smile he heard in her voice unnerved him.

"Take my coat."

"No thanks." She reached past him to pet Ganymede. "I'll just zip up my own."

Chapter Seven

Priorities

By noon that day, the McDonald lot was littered with press copters. By evening, world-wide TV and radio services and late editions of newspapers were disseminating various interpretations of the events believed to have transpired near Jupiter. The New York Times headlined the story SECOND JOVIAN 'COMET' IS MAN-MADE DEVICE, and reported:

FORT DAVIS, TX—A second "comet-like" anomaly in the vicinity of Jupiter was reported yesterday by scientists at McDonald Observatory, in the Davis Mountains of West Texas.

The discovery was made by Dr. Willis Dubin and Dr. David Trombatore who submitted their data for scrutiny by the observatory's staff and also by former NASA scientist Dr. William Reid and astronaut Norman (Bud) Sullivan. According to Dr. Dubin, the object "is or was atomic powered and extraordinarily energetic. The radio-telescope discovery occurred in the 21-megahertz region, a common band for discoveries of natural phenomena; but a later search of an area ahead of the visible comet-like trail revealed an almost surely man-made signal in the VHF range at 231.7 megahertz. As yet the content of the signal, if indeed there is content to it, has not been deciphered."

Asked if the power burst might represent a rocket's initial thrust, Dr. Trombatore speculated: "Such a burst would have been required to free a rocket of Jupiter's gravity, assuming we have accurately calculated the object's pre-blast orbital velocity. But the impact upon any occupants or instruments must have been on the order of 22 G's, an acceleration *our* passengers and instruments could not tolerate. The burst itself, incidentally, if it was non-destructive, exceeds that of any known atomic engine."

Other newspapers were less dispassionate. The Bay Area Observer heralded: JUPITER UFO IDENTIFIED! The youth-oriented Weekly News of the Universe proclaimed: PUTT-PUTT COMET STRIKES AGAIN! Other and even more presumptuous headlines screamed: NEW ATOMIC WEAPON TESTED IN DEEP SPACE?...LIFE FOUND ON JUPITER...SOLAR SYSTEM INVADED?...WILL EARTH BE NEXT VICTIMS? Speculation continued well into the summer months. Most reputable representatives of the scientific community continued to claim that they had no new information and hence were unavailable for comment.

But the Fourth Estate abhors a vacuum, and while few news services stooped to inventing facts, many picked up whatever they could, from wherever they could, regardless of the sanity of the source. When Leon T. Hillary's quarterly newsletter, "Twenty-One," became available in early July, every news service in the world carried quotes from it. Hillary was a famous eccentric millionaire, after all, and had many followers and critics. In his open letter to subscribers, Hillary said:

Dear friends, I was present at McDonald Observatory the night of the second Great Discovery. There I remained never sleeping, for 75 hours, while data was pouring in. Scientists are perplexed, but the story is as plain as it is inspiring:

Last February mankind received its first message from its creators. The glorious signal was repeated again and again with mathematical regularity. What could this first contact have been—if not an alerting signal, a beacon? It meant, "Greetings," and "May we have your attention?"

Then an orbiting observatory saw what appeared to be a comet—where no comet had any business being. *This was the sign in the sky that we were meant to see!*

Seven weeks later another intragalactic chariot paused at our mystical planetary giant and again saluted us with a burst from its unthinkably powerful rockets. This time your humble servant was there to see the sign itself—a tiny pinscratch light near Jupiter, as viewed directly through the eyepiece of the NASA-McDonald telescope! I was awed.

Our great Harvard-Hillary radio telescope tracked it, followed the path it seemed to be taking, and received a short time later a clearly encoded message on a television frequency. The transmission—Dr. William Reid tells us in the June 2 NASA bulletin—was so powerful it could cross interstellar distances!

They are coming; they are coming; they are coming!

Pray that they find us worthy children when they arrive to guide us to our utopian future.

Due to Hillary's mention of him, many members of the press next descended upon Dr. William Reid who, they easily learned, had returned to the NASA staff headquartered at the Center in Houston. His present task involved breaking the mysterious VHF "alien" code.

The NASA Press Relations department happily made available all of the compiled material from Reid's office but, as none of it reached any conclusion or made any prediction, only the technical and scientific journals published any of it. The popular press relied upon the same June 2 NASA house-organ Hillary had quoted, where the following paragraphs also appeared:

Meanwhile, NASA's popular invisible man, Dr. William Reid, is at work night and day trying to decipher that mysterious code. We managed to get out of him one cautiously delivered quote: "I'm going under the assumption that the transmission is a television picture with accompanying sound; but every type of scanning I've tried gives me only meaningless blobs or a gray tone. I haven't even been able to separate sound from picture data. But the work is exciting, because I'm now certain that there is *something* there, something that was intended to be reproduced. Why don't you go check with Gari over in the computer department; she's been working on our latest frames for the past several days."

We asked Bill, excuse it, William, if there was any hope of a resurrection of the Starprobe Relay project. "There's hope," he said. Whatever that means.

We checked with Gari Copalin, image-enhancement engineer, as William had suggested. She gave us only a disgruntled shrug. Ms. Copalin, incidentally, will be *Dr.* Copalin on July 20, when she will be awarded her PhD. Her thesis was on enhancement as accomplished through x, y, and z polarization in liquid crystal photo-grid systems. Nice to know she's working with William on this problem.

In August, the "putt-putt comet" fired up again. "Clearly the same machine we've had two previous sightings of," said an OO-IX astronomer quoted in Science News. "Obviously this is from yet another of the vehicles in a fleet that so far numbers *four*," said another astronomer quoted on the CBS evening news. The most recent "comet" had been found not much beyond the distance of Mars; "and no rocket we know of," explained the lady astronomer on PBS, "could have traveled so far so fast. It's a different ship," she concluded. "For my money," an astronomer at Kitt Peak told RBS radio, "they are probably all natural phenomena. There's an incredible lack of knowledge about even our own solar system."

William Reid was cornered by two reporters as he slipped out of his lab to go to the bathroom. He shrugged, resigned himself to the inevitable, and told them this: "I think there are two vessels; and I think one of them just made a course-corrective burn—pretty much the move I expected it to make, assuming it is heading for earth.

"Now I guess we wait to see if the second vessel burns fuel at approximately the same location, allowing for the seven weeks' difference in their trajectories."

"When do you predict they'll arrive?"

Reid screwed his face into a speculative expression and said, "Next spring."

Some of the services that picked up these quotes and passed them along added that Reid's Starprobe Relay project, still technically under the NASA administrative umbrella, was to be represented before the Industrial Philanthropic Community, Inc. with a plea for funds. It was cynically suggested that with the alien scare, Reid's timing couldn't be better.

On September 12, soon after Congress had resumed following its summer recess, this item appeared in the Washington Post:

WASHINGTON, D.C.—Hotels and other accommodations in the Washington-Baltimore area are full to overflowing as hundreds of thousands of followers of Leon Hillary continue to flood into the nation's Capital. Their mission was beginning to take some shape at nightfall when great crowds were gathering on the Mall and around the Washington Monument. Many of them carried banners and placards hand-lettered, "Fling wide the gates." They were orderly, happily singing folk tunes and old camping songs, and they were generally friendly though not talkative with reporters.

In the Senate Chamber the next morning, the visitors' gallery was overflowing with believers who were softly humming "There's a Long Long Trail A-Winding" in rather shakey three-part harmony. Senators gossiped noisily among themselves as they arrived to take their chairs; they looked up at the gallery from time to time and now and again pointed to the remote-controlled TV cameras fixed to the walls and the gallery rail, cameras which already blinked their on-the-air lights.

The Junior Senator from Wyoming, acting as this day's presiding officer, declared the Senate in session; and with the fall of the gavel the gallery choir instantly became silent. It took longer for the Senators to arrest their private conversations and face front. The call of the calendar was dispensed with as usual; but before morning business could be introduced, the Floor Leader for the Democrats, Daniel Copalin of New York, rose and addressed the assembly:

"I trust we have all received epistles—both earnest and hysterical— explaining the position of faith held by those awaiting the second coming of their gods; but isn't there some particular reason for this visit by such surprisingly large numbers? Can any of you honorable ladies and gentlemen shed any light?"

To those who knew the artful Senator his ploy was patent: he hoped to flush out their foolish business quickly and get rid of them. There were scattered chuckles and muffled guffaws from the Senate floor.

Clayton Ramsey, Republican, Senior Senator from the State of Texas, rose, shrugged, and said, "I hoped nobody would ask. I can shed some light, and I apologize for the dramatic timing—if that's what this is. Their letter of explanation arrived by very punctual messenger only this morning. The letter is signed by many thousands, and the John Hancock at the top of the list is Leon Hillary's. We've heard most of this before, I'm sure, but I suppose I should read it and ask if further discussion is desired." He lifted the letter to hide a yawn, then read:

"'To the Honorable Clayton Wright Ramsey of Texas and members of the United States Senate. While the scientific community is still not in accord on the matter,

79

many respected men of science do agree that it is only a matter of months until we will be visited by alien beings from the far reaches of space. I quote Dr. William Reid of NASA who said in a published interview that the two ships are likely to arrive "next spring." This being the case, we, the millions now awaiting your decision just outside the walls of the Capitol and the untold millions more across the land, wish to call some practical matters to your attention and ask for your prompt action.

"'First, whether the aliens prove to be of a race superior or inferior to our own, should we not pave the way for their arrival, send them signs that we greet them eagerly and with great respect and curiosity? Second, while it might be claimed that any expensive undertaking along these lines ought to be privately paid for, is it not the official duty of any government to welcome official visitors? Third, while we of faith consider the possibility absurd, is it not clear that others will want to take cognizance of any military implications in the arrival of strangers to our world? Is it not vital that we do all in our power to inform the aliens that ours is a peaceful planet? Fourth, should not the government place itself in a position to be able to reassure the population that all is well and is in hand—to avert any attacks on our visitors by frightened zealots in this and other countries?

"'We respectfully submit that these are the issues which deserve the utmost priority, and we eagerly await the announcement of your plan of positive action.' " Senator Ramsey laid the paper on his desk and held up a fat sheaf of pages. "And here are their signatures. Does that answer your question, Senator Copalin?"

There was scattered laughter and a few audible comments.

"Oh, indeed it does," replied the Senator from New

York. "There is only one thing I feel obliged to comment on; Dr. Reid was inappropriately quoted. I have had occasion to speak with the young scientist. He does find some evidence to support the possibility of the arrival 'next spring' of two spacefaring mechanical devices, but he is not at all convinced that they will be carrying passengers nor that they are of alien origin." Copalin tossed a hand in the air in a grand gesture of dismissing the whole subject.

A collective gasp escaped from the gallery as it occurred to them what might happen. Neither Senator Copalin nor Senator Ramsey had introduced the letter as a topic for discussion; it was merely used to answer Senator Copalin's indifferent question. Their plea could be killed here and now—before having even the opportunity to be expanded, contracted, shelved, tabled or shredded.

"On to other matters?" the Chairman asked, nodding toward the formidable pile of computer paper stacked before him.

The Junior Senator from Illinois rose; before speaking she stood for a moment absently tapping her lower lip. "I feel obliged to remind this body that these people represent a sizeable and wide-spread minority in the electorate; and while there is certainly controversy concerning these two space ships, the group has its right to be heard. You know, they are not crackpots. I have spoken with some of them. Their evidence for their beliefs might not satisfy a laboratory scientist; but it is based on certain unexplained phenomena discovered by archeologists, statistics accepted by practically all the astronomers, and volume after volume of alleged eye-witness accounts of previous alien visitations. In fact, they have more of what you'd call *concrete* evidence than ever supported the faith of the

Christians, the Jews, the Buddhists and so on. I recommend they be treated with more respect than—" she gestured off-handedly toward Senator Copalin "—a summary dismissal gives them."

The men and women of the gallery stirred, leaned forward more interestedly, but did not interrupt the Senate with the cheer that might have been expected.

Before the lunch break (after which the gallery was nearly empty), it was decided to create a Subcommittee attached to the Aeronautics and Space Sciences Committee and to instruct the Subcommittee to "stay on top of developments in the matter of mysterious occurrences in outer space that might be linked to the February, April and August 'comet' sightings and apparently associated radio reception."

For the next few weeks, however, there were no further developments.

The media might have let the whole story dwindle were it not for Dr. Reid's unfortunate "next spring" prediction—which no one seemed able to dispute. Apparently the Alienites—as the followers of Leon Hillary were dubbed following the Washington incident—had returned to their homes and jobs and intended to provide no more news copy.

Seven weeks from the third sighting passed, and there was no "sign in the sky" to indicate that the hypothetical second ship had made a course correction similar to the one assumed for the first.

On November 7, the following item was distributed via Associated Press:

NEW YORK CITY—The Industrial Philanthropic Community, Inc., will hold its annual meeting during a charter cruise of the TWA Dolphin, which will depart from its Staten Island mooring on November 28.

The non-profit IPC—which was founded 25 years ago this month in an effort to provide, on a private basis, many of the services being discontinued by government—is expected to hear pleas from such diverse organizations as the United Fund, National Housing for the Disadvantaged, Amalgamated Wine Merchants of America, The Starprobe Relay Project, Leon T. Hillary's newly formed Alien Action Committee, Farm Implements for India, Starving Artists of Paradise, Ltd., and Supplementary Education for Exceptional Children.

Keynote speaker Senator Daniel Copalin will address the IPC on the subject: "Zero Taxation: A Promise to the Twenty-Second Century."

Adhering strictly to their traditional policies, IPC has excluded all members of the press from the junket. Upon return of the Dolphin, on December 9, an open press conference will be held at Radio City in New York. The Dolphin will make a single landing mid-journey at Bermuda.

On November 10, the media carried the enticing but unelaborated announcement that Orbiting Observatory IX and ground-based observatories in China, Australia and the Soviet Union had reported imaging the long-expected second rocket burn of the second mysterious space ship—albeit a number of weeks later than predicted. The OO-IX photograph of the comet-like phenomenon made the November 16 cover of Time.

Chapter 8

On The Dolphin

"Dr. Reid, I'm sorry, but you've exceeded your weight allotment many times over. Surely you must realize that this one crate alone holds more than you're allowed to carry. You'll just have to leave it—"

"Would you do me a favor, please. Have Dr. Gari Copalin paged."

"All right. But you can't pull any strings. These things are absolutes, you know." The unsympathetic clerk reached for her desk intercom. As she did so, she handed William a colorful brochure that, she apparently assumed, spoke with greater authority than she did.

The request for Dr. Copalin to come to the ticket counter reverberated around the geodesic dome of the terminal, mingling with the echoes of voices, soft music, and foot traffic on the marble floor.

"She hasn't boarded already, has she?" William asked the clerk.

The clerk checked her passenger list. "No," she answered.

William lifted his suitcase off the scales.

The clerk reprimanded: "You can't leave your *clothes* behind!"

He saw Gari and Bud approaching with a handcart of luggage. Gari waved and yelled, "Got held up in traffic."

"They're keeping us to the weight limit," William announced. Unintentionally, he summoned a number of reporters.

"Have you seen Greitzer?" Gari asked.

"No; do you think he can help?"

Gari hefted her suitcases from the cart and set them on the floor. Bud placed another heavy crate on the scales alongside William's three.

Bud addressed the clerk: "Listen, sweetheart, some exceptions have to be made. Can you get ahold of the flight manager. Or better—the president of the company?"

The girl's eyebrows went up and she smiled as if she were trying not to. "You're Bud Sullivan, aren't you?"

He nodded grandly. "What's your name?"

"Cynthia. Listen, Bud, I'll call anybody you say; but I can't let more than 35 kilos per person on board. I don't think anybody can, really, because every passenger I've checked in so far has gone the limit. I've never seen so much audio-visual equipment and big charts and posters and things. What's in these crates anyway—gold bricks?"

Gari interposed: "More audio-visual equipment. Could you step on it? There's a line forming behind us, and I'd rather not have to hold things up."

The girl was winding up to put the pushy lady scientist in her place when Bud smiled and said, "Please?"

The "line" forming behind and around them consisted

85

mostly of reporters who were hastily scribbling notes. They noted the approximate size and shape of the crates in question, saw the official NASA emblem on all four of them, and tried to make out other hand-scribbled labels.

By the time the flight manager had arrived to apologize and stand by the clerk's no-overweight decision, Gari had rounded up a number of friends and acquaintances, including Dr. Greitzer, Dr. Clark, and Dr. Hanley of NASA, and her father, Senator Copalin.

The Senator appealed to the flight manager's interest in matters of mysterious importance. "I sympathize with your position entirely," the Senator finally said reluctantly; "but I must ask a special favor of you. These crates are vitally needed on the Dolphin, and, as there seems to be only one way to get them on, would you be so kind as to send an attendant into the baggage room and have him withdraw the larger of my two suitcases; we'll leave it behind and credit the weight of it to that which Dr. Reid has to carry."

The reporters were dumbfounded. "Good God," one of them said a trifle too loudly.

The other scientists assembled performed similar gestures—either lightening a case or leaving one or more behind altogether.

The Senator walked with William, Gari and Bud toward the boarding gate. He turned to them and said wryly, "Your presentation had better be good. It looks like I'll be attending it in my pajamas."

"You don't know what's in the crates?" William asked.

Gari answered for her father: "No. I haven't told him anything. He trusts me."

Not since the Dolphin's maiden voyage almost four years ago had so much furor been generated by a single flight. Reporters and cameramen, forbidden to set foot aboard the Dolphin, watched from prime locations, many of them airborne in helicopters. Millions of New Yorkers hurried into Battery Park and lined the parkways on either side of the East River; they ferried to the Statue of Liberty, crowded onto Ellis and Governor's Islands, and rimmed the walkway on the newly completed lowest level of the Verrazano Narrows bridge.

Although this was the Dolphin's twelfth departure from its cavernous Staten Island home, the Islanders turned out again in force to take up their superior locations right at the mouth of the hangar. At 4:00 in the afternoon, precisely, when the sun was low and golden and the wind was cold, they cheered as the hangar doors were rolled back. They cheered again when the familiar silver-gray downtipped nose came out into the light and the echoing hiss of the Dolphin's eight jets began to rise in pitch. When the whole of its 425-meter length was visible and its tail fins had cleared the hangar, there arose another cheer; and a rocket exploded prematurely over Battery Park spraying confetti and streamers over Upper New York Bay.

Taxiing majestically toward Manhattan, its smooth skin of titanium-alloy-foam burning with sunlight, the Dolphin sprayed out its ballast and began to rock gently in the water as cells containing 328,000 cubic meters of helium made their capability known.

The leviathan dirigible—longer than the height of a World Trade Center tower and containing approximately the same volume—slipped gracefully and almost silently into the air. With its gently curved tail fins and small ventral wings, its downtipped nose and its sleek body glistening with droplets of mist, the Dolphin looked rather like the aquatic mammal from which it got its name.

Copters flitted like dragonflies around the impossible metal balloon, and a swarm of pleasure boats on the bay followed the Dolphin into the mouth of the East River. Confetti-and-streamer rockets burst from everywhere. Passengers of the Dolphin lined the windows of the observation gondola and waved to the earth that was slowly dropping away; and, as the airship floated over the East River, observers on the ever-diminishing bridges waved back.

William Reid and Gari Copalin missed most of this spontaneous ceremony. As soon as they had determined that the crates had been placed in William's cabin, they had gone there to unpack their "audio-visual" instruments and make them operational.

"Do you know what's in those crates, by the way?" Senator Copalin asked.

Bud Sullivan nodded. "I'm sure they'll tell you if you ask them."

The Senator shrugged, as if to say: I suppose they'll tell me of their own accord if they want me to know. It was clear that Bud did not feel free to divulge the information.

They were in the Moonshadows Bar, in the prow of the Dolphin, through the windows of which they could keep a lazy eye on the glistening sea under a fat crescent moon. There was a ship down there, no bigger than a good-sized yacht, which seemed to be matching the Dolphin's moves. It too was a subject of occasional and lazy curiosity. It had been with them since nightfall, perhaps since the airship had passed over the New York coast.

Leon Hillary sat down on the other side of Bud. To avoid having to converse with him, Bud said the first thing that came into his head to the Senator. "What's the

88

capacity of the Dolphin? Do you know?"

"In passengers? I've been told it's 328, with 48 support personnel and a flight crew of five. Beautiful ship, isn't it. Tranquilizing. Tranquility, I'm assured, is its chief attraction. Buy you a drink?"

"Thanks, yes—dry Rob Roy. Why are you here, incidentally? I mean, I'm not complaining, but who sent you?"

The Senator laughed. "The Senate. There's a rep from the House here too. Advisors, mostly. To make sure nothing contrary to government policy is acted upon. It's a vacation for me."

Hillary took advantage of the interruption caused by drinks arriving; he rested a hand in comradely fashion on Bud's forearm.

"I need to chat a spell with you, Bud," he rumbled.

Copalin leaned around and said to Hillary, "Pardon me, Leon, I hope you'll let me have Bud a while longer. There are things *I* need to talk to him about."

"Why sure," Hillary said grinning. "Didn't mean to butt in on family matters." He stepped off his bar stool and ambled toward three men seated at a corner table.

"You've got something on your mind," Bud said to the Senator. "It's beginning to make me nervous. What's up?"

Copalin was still looking at Hillary. "Can't stand that man," he confessed. "I'm glad he and I don't often agree politically. Do you like Bill Reid, son?"

Bud laughed. "Better call him William to his face. He's got a harmless perfectionist streak. Yes, I like him very much. He's a brilliant scientist and engineer—and a very good man. Dense sometimes, though. If there's something developing between him and Gari, he might be the last to know it."

89

The Senator smiled unsettlingly. "If?"

"Oh, I know there's something. They haven't said anything to me."

"What do you think of his Starprobe, Bud? Like the idea? Caught up in the romance of it?"

"Yeah. But I've wondered what I'd do if funds that could send me into space were rechanneled to Starprobe. It's not *that* important. Not compared to the Delta Colony."

"Like it out there, do you?"

Bud nodded, momentarily drifting back into space in his memory.

"I take it you're here to assist with the Starprobe presentation. When is it?"

"Thursday, but William's trying to get it postponed till after Bermuda."

"I doubt he'll be able to. Bermuda's the mid-point. The IPC Committee hears pleas for the first half of the trip and uses the second half for its own deliberations. There'll be no presentations after Bermuda."

"Could they make the change with your help?"

"I don't know. Why is it important?"

"There will be reporters at Bermuda pumping everybody who steps off this airship."

"Yes, that's to be expected. So?"

"I think you'd better talk to Gari."

"Can't Dr. Reid speak for himself?"

"Well, yes, if it occurs to him."

The bartender leaned closer. "Another round for you gentlemen?"

The Senator deferred to Bud, who stared out at the thin smears of clouds, the moon-lighted sea, the miniscule lights on the yacht that seemed to be following them—and answered dully, "Yeah, why not?"

An event occurred on the third day out which served to focus attention even more on the perpetually absent Dr. Reid. Senator Copalin was a guest at an informal morning session between presentations and was fielding questions concerning his keynote address.

A woman from the Edison Company had the floor. "I admire you for the sheer scope of your dream, Senator, but I feel compelled to ask you how for example, one could finance the system of courts, police and the military— *voluntarily*? I see us lapsing into anarchy in just the attempt."

The Senator, immaculately dressed, supremely confident, smiled and said, "I'm not the philosopher of law you need to ask that of. Some of the same measures in use today for other social programs would doubtless be applied—lotteries, sweepstakes, bond issues, fund-raising drives—but whether or not our Constitution as well, presently constituted, would allow for a complete separation of government and economy . . . I don't know. My whole thesis, really, is just that we should set such a society as our goal. Unless it becomes official, we can never be certain that present trends won't be reversed, probably in the face of some alleged emergency. Of course we can *tolerate* our present tax average of seven percent. If you'll recall, our great grandparents were tolerating a taxation of almost 70 percent! Fortunately, their children did not. Consequently, a decline in taxation set in—accidentally, for all practical purposes. Accidentally, I say because there was no philosophical basis for it consciously set up in the minds of the voting public. It was seen as a pragmatic solution to the problem of a stagnant country devouring itself, not as a noble goal."

"Senator," a man asked, rising, fumbling for words,

"What do you predict would be the future of organizations like our own IPC under total economic freedom? I mean, we like to think of ourselves as generous benefactors of mankind, but I wonder—would we be so generous if each act of beneficence did *not* carry a tax-writeoff along with it? In a way, it's the very heinous taxes you speak of that keep *us* in business, as it were."

There was scattered knowing laughter.

"Let that be your homework assignment," the Senator suggested with a grin. "It seems to me that you people are the very ones to come up with an answer to that."

The morning's moderator stepped to the dais. "I'm terribly sorry to have to cut this short, Senator, ladies and gentlemen, but I have just been informed by CBS in New York that a newsbreak is now beginning that might have some bearing on a subject of our deliberation." As he spoke, a projection screen was coming out of the ceiling behind him. "I'm sure we all appreciate the kind words of Senator Copalin. . . ."

Not many of those in his audience accepted the Senator's thesis whole-cloth, but he received the enthusiastic ovation owed to a respected thinker and charismatic public speaker.

The video beam from a projection booth at the rear of the auditorium sent its picture before the screen was fully down. "Interesting development for all you UFO bugs and Alienites out there," the newsman said. "The Harvard-Hillary radio telescope late last night was used to transmit a message to the point in space where one of the mysterious space ships has actually been seen. Less than an hour later, the ship *returned* a signal believed to be identical to the disruptive beam first received from outer space. . . ."

An annoying flood of light entered the auditorium as

the door at the rear was yanked open. Several in the audience turned, mostly out of reflex, and saw silhouetted there a medium-sized man and a very small woman.

"...and an hour and seven minutes later," the newsman continued, "another signal was beamed from the space ship. This new signal is believed to be like, in character, the second type of signal received earlier from either this or the other mysterious ship. Curiouser and curiouser!"

There was nothing further of consequence. When the report was concluded and the lights were again coming up in the auditorium, William Reid—unshaven, in wrinkled clothing and tattered tennis shoes—ran down the aisle to where the moderator stood. Reid said, loudly enough for all to hear, "How can I obtain a copy of the data from McDonald?"

"*I* don't know," the moderator said, miffed at being asked. "Perhaps you can call for it to be transmitted to you here. Maybe they'll send it to Bermuda. *I* can't help you."

William met Gari by the rear door and muttered, "We're trapped on this damned flying fish. I've got to get that data."

Gari laughed. "Then we'll get it," she said as they hurried into the corridor.

Getting it was not easy. All the outgoing telephone calls that could be handled by the Dolphin's plex board were being handled, and there was a waiting list for channels. Reid placed his name on the list and was told that he would have to wait two or three hours at best. Even worse, all calls were being limited to five minutes; and a full transmission of all of McDonald's data was sure to take longer than that.

William and Gari waited impatiently in the Moonshadows Bar. Their minds were racing along similar paths and on occasion one of them would make a remark; minutes later the other would reply or make a seemingly unrelated statement.

"There are four separate signals per frame," said William.

"Has anyone ever transmitted a hologram?" Gari asked.

"Yes," William responded. "But I don't think so."

"Seven square decimeters," Gari muttered. "Exactly."

William's right leg bounced nervously. Gari laid her hand on it to make him stop.

William rose and stood by one of the broad windows.

"Gari," he said after a few minutes, "come here. What do you suppose all that activity is for?"

Under a noontime sun in a hazy sky, dozens of copters were keeping pace with the Dolphin. Below on the blinding sea there were as many ships and boats. Gari shook her head, as puzzled as William was.

When a copter swung close enough to be peered into, however, they saw two men inside talking to little black boxes.

"Telephone relays!" Gari and William said to each other at the same time.

"But why, I wonder?" William asked.

"*I* don't know," Gari said, mimicking the man in the auditorium. "But some people on the Dolphin must be in contact with them. That's a way we could get our message out and the data in."

"How do we find out who—?" William wondered aloud.

The bartender looked around surreptitiously, stepped close to Gari and William, reduced his voice almost to a whisper, and asked, "Are you Dr. Reid, by any chance?"

William nodded, unable to imagine what this man wanted of him.

"Can I trust you and the lady not to ask me any questions? Absolutely none?" Before waiting for a reply, he produced a telephone from his vest pocket.

"Yes!" Gari whispered loudly.

The bartender spoke softly into his phone. "I have Dr. Reid here. He needs to place an emergency call. Will you help him?"

The answer came back at once: "Of course, put him on."

Hillary had come to Bud's cabin. He leaned against the rounded-square porthole frame—beyond which could be seen only night blackness—and waited for Bud's decision.

"How can I, Leon?" Bud asked; he was seated at the cabin's small pull-down desk. "Greitzer has me roped into his presentation to get funds for a 30-meter optical telescope he wants to build and man at Delta; and there's Starprobe, of course. I can't very well try the patience of those good people by coming before them a third time— on *your* behalf. What can I help you with anyway? Those big shots aren't bowled over by a rocket jockey. Are they?"

Hillary waited, smiling slightly.

"I'll tell you, though, I am convinced we're about to meet some genuine aliens."

The cowboy smiled a little more broadly. He took out a cigar.

"If you promise not to light that thing in here, I'll give you this much. I'll tell them I agree with you that aliens are coming—as long as you don't expect me to endorse that nutty religion of yours."

"I admire idealism in a man, Gari," her father said; "I consider myself quite an idealist, in fact. But your friend Dr. Reid puzzles me. His head seems to be a thousand years in the future. He seems to be *only* an idealist. Is he afraid of the present?"

She laughed. "God, you can ask aggravating questions! I wish I knew. I really wish I knew."

They sat at a table set for four on the dining terrace of Shinbone Alley, an out-of-the-way restaurant overlooking the port of Hamilton, in the Bermudas. The warm breeze carried not even a suggestion of the early-winter chill of New York. The Dolphin was out there sleeping at the end of the longest pier, its silver-gray mass stretching across the turquoise water toward the open sea.

Gari resurrected a memory. "He's told me he has never understood 'social' motivations. To him what's right is right, and he can't understand why others can't see it. Compromise, vested interests, pragmatic decisions, anything he would regard as blatantly unscientific thinking—they frighten him in some way."

"Are you in love with him?"

"Yes."

"Told Bud?"

Gari smiled a twisted smile. "I've been hoping to convince William first. And you should wait your turn. I don't know why I'm talking so much—must be tired."

"You don't seem tired to me, ebullient in fact."

A grinning tourist approached their table. He was dressed in white slacks, a tropical-floral shirt and a floppy reed hat. He removed his dark glasses as he sat down. It was William. He laughed at Gari's surprised expression and said, "I gave 'em the slip. The boutique owner let me out the back way while the reporters were dozing in front. How do I look?"

"Like somebody else," said Gari, "but kinda nice. Fresh."

"Seen Bud?" the Senator asked. "He's late."

"Is he joining us? I haven't seen him, not since the Hillary presentation yesterday." William's face had abruptly lost its cherriness to an expression of thoughtful anger. "He shouldn't have done that."

The Senator shrugged. "At least his endorsement of Hillary wasn't public."

"Yes it was," William said. "That airship is swarming with people in touch with the press. That's why that armada's following the Dolphin. A reporter at the boutique asked me, 'What will you tell the IPC?' Not what *did* you tell them. They already knew you got my session postponed until the flight resumes in the morning."

Bud appeared with a bang as his sandals hit the wood floor of the outdoor terrace; he had vaulted over the railing at the cantilevered edge. A woman at a nearby table uttered a startled cry. Bud's famous green eyes were shaded, but his athletic build, distinctive reddish hair and overpublicized face made him easily recognizable. As he approached, then pulled out his chair and sat, he said to Copalin: "Leave it to a politician to pick a restaurant nobody's ever heard of"; to Gari: "Morning, lover"; and facetiously to William: "My name's Bud Sullivan, I don't believe we've met."

"Hi, Bud," said Gari.

Bud's face fell. "What's wrong?" When no one seemed eager to answer him, he added: "Tell me. I'm an adult. And I love all of you."

"Hillary," William said flatly.

It took Bud a second to understand. "But surely you don't think that I—"

"Do you want that man in charge of things when the

97

aliens arrive?" Gari asked Bud.

"Weren't you there at the presentation yesterday?" Bud asked earnestly. "I made my position clear, and I did not mention the work you guys are doing." It was obvious Bud was affected by his friends' implicit accusation. "I'm still on your side, you know. I'll give it all I've got tomorrow." He added, by way of a plea for understanding: "You act like I sold my soul to the devil!"

The Senator watched the three young people intently, without entering the conversation.

William said sadly, "You did."

"Oh come on!" said Bud. "Hillary's right and you know it. There are aliens coming to earth, and we do have to prepare for them!

"How?" Gari asked. "By building shrines?"

"I can't have you representing Starprobe now," William said to Bud. "It would link us to that lunatic. I'm sorry."

"Oh, don't do this, Billy Boy—William," Bud pleaded, his deep hurt showing nakedly. "You know I didn't choose Hillary's way over yours." He suddenly realized: "But it sure will look that way if you kick me out of your camp now!"

Gari and her father both looked searchingly at William.

"I'm sorry," William reiterated, looking intently into his friend's eyes.

Bud picked up the menu. "Do you suppose their oyster cocktail is any good?" He dropped the menu back onto the table. "I'm sorry too," he said. "I'll see you back on the Dolphin. Excuse me." He left by the door.

The Senator asked William, "Don't you think he could have been an asset anyway?"

William shook his head. "Not in the long run. Besides,

we don't need anything more than our pictures. That's where the truth lies. They won't turn us down; they *can't* now."

William began his presentation by showing the exquisite Starprobe animation NASA had commissioned several years previously.

While a narrator talked of light speeds, broadcast and reception ranges, solar and stellar winds, and dates that led deep into an unformed future....

A space tug released its cargo, a bristling instrument package ... arms on it opened and sails began to unfold and unfold and unfold until the instrument itself was out of sight at the horizon of a field of silver ... in a closeup of the instrument, a propulsion pod telescoped out, ignited, and began to position and propel the incredible kite with a steady blue stream of ions ... the kite receded until the whole octagonal shape of the sail assembly was in the picture and the instrument was only a black dot in the center ... the octagon receded until it was no more than a minor star moving through the galaxy ... another tug was readied for launch ... another instrument and sail assembly trailed after the first ... a fleet of Starprobes grew farther and farther apart, broadcasting our greeting, relaying any replies back to earth, picking up speed, seeking out the galaxy core.

Reading from prepared notes, William told his interested audience what the initial and operating costs would be and stressed the options that would open up in years to come, when new and better methods and machinery would be available. With roughly annual launches, he explained, even if the project were to be discontinued after only three probes, a clear relay of information would continue for nearly three hundred

99

years. "Any schoolboy today can quote you the statistics suggesting that there might be a million civilizations out there. Over the past 60 years, planets have been found orbiting 23 of our neighboring stars, and it is believed that a number of these could be biologically similar to earth. But all of this is still theory." William placed the last of his notes on the podium. "However, today you will be shown some facts."

He glanced to the table next to him where Gari was completing the assembly of a 1.5-meter photo-grid, connecting its cable to a computer unit. She nodded and smiled.

"I want to show you the results of work Dr. Copalin and I have been doing with signals that came from those two mysterious space vehicles heading toward earth. I believe what you are about to see will reinforce my contention that something like Starprobe is not only desirable but necessary. Also, I need your help. A few rational statements from highly respected people, such as yourselves, might help avert sensationalism, presumption, and possibly panic—when this material becomes readily available. If I had taken this to government officials first, the press would have had it instantly. I must also pass along my request for sanity to any press services eavesdropping now. I am convinced that even though a good many phones have been confiscated in the past 24 hours, we are probably being heard, perhaps even seen, by the outside world. We still have our unexplained escort of ships and copters out there, and I doubt that their interest is merely in the beauty of the Dolphin's flight."

Liquid crystal dots on the photo-grid changed color and brightness at random at first, then settled on a medium gray. Out of the gray a black-and-white picture emerged.

"Without enhancement, the incoming picture looked like this. The central figure there looks much like a man out of focus standing before a picturephone." The picture became sharper. "This next frame resulted from our asking the computer to seek out the midpoints in the gradations of smears and to strike a hard line in place of the soft one." The figure was evidently an animal of some kind with eyes, mouth and hair where one would expect to find them, but the eyes were too round and too wide-set, and the head was too tall. "In the next frame you'll see results of further enhancement and also from varying the condensation of the signal."

There were audible gasps from the men and women of the IPC, who had already begun to murmur among themselves. They were looking at an alien being. On the creature's hand, partially obscuring its face, each of the five fingers were subdivided midway, making ten fingertips. One could see what appeared to be moisture collected in beads below the hair line.

Out of the rising furor in the auditorium, someone asked loudly, "Can you convince us these pictures are neither accidental nor a hoax?"

"I hope so. All of our data is here for you to examine during the remainder of the voyage. You may ask for confirmation from McDonald Observatory. And many scientists have copies of the original recordings, against which you may compare our results."

"Why haven't other scientists produced these pictures then?"

"You'll have to ask them."

Gari cleared her throat.

William smiled at her. "There's more," he told his spellbound listeners. "Each frame contains so much picture data that one may choose one's perceptible depth of field. Compare this aspect roughly to our phone plex boards, which can subdivide a frequency almost infinitely, in theory anyway." He nodded to Gari.

She typed instructions into the display unit. The figure on the screen became fuzzy; behind it there was a column on which there were instruments; it came into focus. The instrument column began to become less distinct and a whole background scene emerged: the floor under the creature was a ribbon platform of some kind which curved upward in the distance; on it were arranged numerous clusters of instruments at which were stationed "men." In the darkness to the right and left of the aisle were streaks which suggested massive machinery.

"What do you suppose those little creatures on the floor are? Scavengers?" asked a white-haired little lady who stood to pose the question. Her sweet soft voice placed her more at a garden club than among the august and powerful.

"That's an interesting thought," said William. "I don't know."

"There is no doubt in your mind that we are seeing inside an alien ship?" asked a man with a lazy drawl.

"Very little," William answered.

"You must forgive us if we are not so easily convinced," the moderator, standing next to William, said. "There are grave implications here for philosophers, scientists, perhaps for our military to be cognizant of."

"There was no sound with these pictures?" The questioner's voice was loud and rough; it belonged to Leon Hillary who stood at the rear.

"We assume there must be," William answered, "but we have not yet resolved anything better than static."

"Excuse me," said a man not much older than William, "Dr. Reid, have you any affiliation with Mr. Hillary?"

"None, because I do not believe Hillary and his followers have any affiliation with reality. They would be expressing the same notions if all we were dealing with were an irregularity in the aurora borealis. Their roots are in superstitious dogma on the order of astrology. I think it would be a cruel misrepresentation to offer them the privilege of speaking for the human race should the aliens arrive."

The moderator said quietly to William: "One IPC presenter may not attack another. This is not a platform for debate. If this happens again, you will be disqualified and asked to leave the dais."

An elderly gentleman rose from the front row and headed for the door, muttering, "This is unconscionable. A circus. A fraud and a criminal interruption of our work."

Two men, close allies apparently, followed him out.

The garden-club woman asked William, "Is there more you can show us at this time? You implied there were other pictures."

William's mouth was open in astonishment. He looked from the moderator to the door through which the men had departed, to the woman who had just spoken. "What? Oh, yes, there are other pictures," he said shakily.

He answered occasional questions—some interested, some skeptical—as he showed the rest of what he and Gari had prepared.

How does Bud do it? William wondered; how can he stand before an audience of skeptics and speak with such confidence and lack of concern? How would he have handled this? Should I have asked him to make this presentation? Why didn't he come to listen?

William would have felt some moral support, at least, if he had known that Bud was watching, studying the audience, approving of William's performance, from behind the glass ports of the projection booth at the back of the room.

The Dolphin had left the warm calm of Gulf Stream waters and was being rocked, like a ship on the sea, by fierce winter winds. One day out of New York the IPC Committee distributed their decisions. The verdicts came in a crude package: phonetically spelled from a voice-activated printer, on tissue-thin paper, sealed but unwrapped and unribboned.

Bud burst into William's cabin, their conflicts forgotten for the moment. "We got the telescope!" he babbled; "to the tune of eighteen billion—for PR, prestige, and advertising. It will be called the IPC-Delta Installation!"

William and Gari were sitting on the bed.

"Good," William said warmly but distantly.

Bud frowned. "You only got a partial?" he guessed, appalled at the idea.

"Starprobe got a no," Gari said flatly.

William handed Bud the folded tissues. "Read it," he said. He grabbed them back before Bud could open the pages. "Here, I'll point out some highlights. Like this word, 'unconvincing,' and here where it says, 'no clear and present need,' and—" he flipped over a page "—this: 'romantically appealing, but impractical.' The IPC admits their vote was almost a tie, and they invite us back next year for another go at it. On the last page, where they give us comments of individual members, unidentified of course, somebody says, 'inspired project which some day must be realized,' and somebody else makes the incredible remark that, 'as long as we are to be visited by traveling aliens, at no cost to ourselves, why spend untold billions to—' and so forth. Here's the last remark; somebody calls

104

it 'a child's dream and a lovely one, but with no chance of any sort of payoff in the forseeable future.' "

Bud heard the unsteadiness of William's voice and felt the depth of William's anger as a knot in his own stomach. "What can I do?" he asked hopelessly.

William shook his head.

"May I come in?" It was Hillary outside the cabin door Bud had left ajar.

"How'd you make out, Leon?" Bud asked.

"A partial. They've granted us something for a feasibility study—a study I've already shelled out for. We know what we want to do and how much it'll cost. Listen, guys, I hope we can pull off some kind of a truce. I have the funds; you are coming up with the intelligence. Can't we get together on this thing?"

William seemed to be functioning on two levels. With tears gleaming in his eyes he looked up and said with uncharacteristic firmness, "No, Mr. Hillary, we can't get together, because we *aren't* together."

"Well, I tried," Hillary said to Bud. He looked down at William and said evenly, shaking his head, "Dumb arrogant son of a bitch. Will you continue to work on the aliens' messages?"

"As long as NASA wants me to," William answered indifferently. "They're paying my salary."

Bud tossed his head gesturing to Hillary that it was time for him to clear out.

Respectfully, Hillary pulled the door gently to behind him.

"Why are you this upset?" Bud asked William. "Did you expect unanimous enthusiasm and consent? Automatic agreement?"

"Of course."

Gari and Bud's eyes met. Each was pleading with the

105

other for some clue, some statement that would help William over his disappointment. At last Bud shrugged and suggested:

"Let's go to the bar."

It was unclear for a minute whether William had not heard the suggestion or was laboriously thinking it over. "Okay," he said, rising from the bed, "but let's not talk. I just want to look out at the storm and let it hypnotize me. I love storms."

"As long as they're not the human kind," Gari gibbed.

The bar was crowded with those celebrating and those drowning their sorrows. The horizon—out beyond the big windows—swayed disorientingly: it was like seeing the stormy sea from a ship but with the motions reversed. Droplets ran almost laterally across the windows which fluttered with gusts of wind, and then froze at the metal edges. Frequent lightning streaks added blue to the brownish gray of the clouds behind which the sun was sinking.

A mad scientist joined their table. Greitzer's hair was a wirey white disarray and his jacket was loose around his boney shoulders, giving him an artificial slouch.

"What'll it be," asked Gari, "champagne or a double martini?"

"Can the two be mixed?" Greitzer asked, laughing. "I'm living with both victories and defeats. We got our Delta scope, we lost Starprobe; we got our Pluto probe, we lost the Mars colony; we got feasibility money for a second energy-satellite factory at Delta, we lost our feasibility for a new artificial colony at L-5. And so on, and so on. And I just was talking to the good Senator, who has convinced me that NASA's days are numbered. Soon, he believes, private corporations will entirely assume all but defense functions, and those will fall under a new contract agency of the DOD. All things considered—a double martini, I guess. And William—"

"You mean there's more?"

"I didn't get money for your continued work with the alien signals. Now don't panic; both Senator Copalin and Representative Prather think there'll be no problem getting funds for you under a defense-grant umbrella. But you're still working for us in any case. The thing is . . . you'll have to work out of McDonald, where facilities are already operating. That is, you'll have to come to terms, somehow, with Hillary. I don't have to tell you, I hope, that I disapprove of his being involved, and that I want you to keep him at arm's length—if possible."

William took a deep breath and let it out. "Let's talk about something else," he suggested.

The waiter put the drinks into the hands of the party because the tabletop was too unsteady.

"There isn't anything else to talk about, is there?" Gari muttered rhetorically.

They stared out at the entertaining, energetic, purposeless storm.

Chapter 9

Prelude and Fugue

February 27, a Sunday, another day when the sun did not set. It allowed the gray sky to fade evenly over the Davis Mountains - as if our star had frozen and unspectacularly had lost its flame.

White fluorescents glowed from the buildings of McDonald Observatory, and sparcely placed homes in the ragged valleys and canyons nearby sparkled with electrical ambers and blues. A phone antenna atop Mount Livermore blinked its red altitude lamps. Northwest of Livermore, the vast Harvard-Hillary radio dish was dull gray in the last of twilight; its web of elements reflected the occasional sheet lightning passively and indifferently. In Madera Canyon, above a grove of ancient wind-strained walnut trees, on a granite ledge, a modern cabin was perched. In it the only illumination came from a flapping, rumbling fire. The fireplace heated one side of Gari's and William's naked bodies; the wind coursing through curved plastiglass doors chilled the other; the carpet beneath them lightly pricked them as they slowly moved. They said nothing because it was as if their minds had become only physical organs; yet they seemed remote from physical sensations because, for them both, such intensity of feeling had previously originated only in imagination. They returned to earth sometime after dark, as if their matter had been teleported back into this ordinary rustic-modern room from elsewhere. A drop of water blew onto William's hand. He raised himself on one elbow.

"Don't get up," she said firmly.

"The rain—"

"Let it. Well, go ahead. We have to get up sooner or later. I'm starved, come to think of it."

Her body glistened in the unsteady orange light. As he rose he moved his hand possessively across her breasts, down her body, her leg.

The concave surface of the door reflected Gari, distorted, as she walked to stand next to William, to look out with him at the lights on the canyon floor and the faint glow around the domes of McDonald.

"What do you suppose they're doing?" he asked.

She followed his sight up to McDonald. At what was probably the edge of the copter lot, a red-orange point of light flashed several times in succession, paused, then flashed again.

She said, "I'm not about to call them and ask. It's just possible they still don't know we're here. Surely we can have a few more days in peace before they find us again." She squeezed his butt. "Think so, Reedly Bill?"

"If we're lucky, Carrie Copland." He returned the squeeze, having to bend lower to do it.

A Sunday comic had recently appeared based loosely

on current events. Its hero and heroine were Reedly Bill and Carrie Copland, top earth scientists in touch with benevolent aliens who were coming to bring us scientific wonders the likes of which we had only dreamed about—telekenesis, matter transportation, cloaks of invisibility, knowledge acquired by swallowing a pill. Reedly and Carrie were pursued by villains of an anti-technology cult who would stop at nothing to destroy earth's benefactors. In reality, William and Gari's pursuers were fairly ordinary citizens, like the creator of that comic strip who wanted "the inside dope, if you know what I mean." Like Hillary and Dr. Dubin, scientists from all over the world had theories to offer (some of them probably valuable, unfortunately). Literally thousands of reporters called daily. Even though they had cross-circuited their phone numbers to go through the Houston NASA board, somehow their whereabouts never stayed secret for long. This cabin—right under McDonald's front porch (and in fact owned by a company owned by a parent company owned by Hillary)—had hidden them for an unusually long time: four days.

Their data from the Hillary radio-telescope was relayed to them unfailingly by Dr. Greitzer, wherever they were. The trick, for William and Gari, was to preserve their solitude long enough to be able to analyze the material.

"How much time?" Gari asked. She scooped her shirt from a chair and picked up her slacks from the floor.

"Don't do it," William said with mock menace.

She dropped the clothes and went naked into the kitchen.

William looked at the digitals built into the polished-granite chimney. "Plenty of time," he answered her.

"If we're dining in the nude, then we're eating at the

glass table," she called out, dimming up the kitchen light.

A whir started by itself in a blue-plastic box beside the music console. William lifted the edge of a long strip of paper that was pouring from it. "It's the report from Japan," he announced loudly. "Nakayama says he doubts that the aliens' symbols are a pictorial language. He thinks they're purely abstract, like an alphabet, because of their arrangement and the fact that they don't repeat exactly even when redundant pictures occur. But he hasn't cracked it either. He wants to meet with us. He'll be in Houston... tomorrow. He—listen to this, Gari—he asks if it's occurred to us that no one seems to be in charge of that alien ship. Nakayama thinks they don't know what they're doing."

Gari laughed. "That would certainly take us off the hook."

"Japan's calling up its military. Nakayama thinks the United States is taking this thing too lightly. Maybe he's got a point. Have you talked to your father lately?"

"I haven't been able to reach him in the last few days. Why? Want to know if *our* military is being called up? I'll try to find out. Wine with your steak?"

"Better not. We've got a long night ahead of us."

A day on the aliens' home planet, it seemed reasonable to assume, must have been 26 hours, 56 minutes and about 40 seconds long; for that had been the spacing of the alien calls to earth for the past 13 days. Each call had lasted precisely 47 minutes and 8 seconds, as if their transmission equipment were on a timer—to be terminated as prearranged.

A number of facilities, besides the Harvard-Hillary-McDonald installation, were capable of two-way talk with the aliens. No one had objected when, the week before, the British Interplanetary Society had taken charge of scheduling—so that each of several scientists could have a portion of the aliens' 47 minutes. But consequently nobody had yet spent enough time, cumulatively, to make much headway with any particular method of communication. One group continued to try musical progressions; another repeated mathematical sequences (the aliens, sure enough, could add and subtract in base 10); also tried were pictorial representations with superimposed nouns written in English, the gesticulative language of the deaf, and so on. Each of these programs was observed by each of the other scientists; and anyone in the world who was interested could watch the entire 47 minutes (sponsored on CBS by General Hydrofuels, Inc.) on a split screen— aliens on the left, earthmen on the right—uninterrupted by commercials.

Tonight's broadcast was expected to begin promptly at 11:10.

William and Gari ate hastily—their romantic interlude so far out of mind that their nudity felt silly. They dressed and were into their second hour studying tapes of previous broadcasts, when Gari's phone (propped beside William's on the mantel, toned. The caller was gossip Celia Thompson.

"How did you get the NASA board to put your call through?" Gari asked her with honest curiosity.

"Oh, I'm not going through NASA, dear. Gleeful as I must sound, I'm really sort of sorry to have to tell you that you've been located again. I'm at McDonald. I have a shade more to confess—now don't cut me off—there's a great line of sight from up here, right into your living room. You're not saying very much, Gari."

"Actions have already spoken louder, apparently."

"The world just has to know about you and your

112

famous co-worker, don't you think? You do sympathize, I'm sure. I'm hoping you'll give me a statement."

Gari was smoldering. She said nothing. Her thumb slowly descended onto the cut-off button and she broke the connection cold-bloodedly, as if performing an execution.

William smiled, but the rest of his expression did little to cheer Gari. "That's what those orange flashes were, I guess. Some kind of telaser camera—infrared. Would she really publish pictures like that?"

Gari named her only serious worry: "We've got to get to Bud before Celia does. She'll probably call him for a comment, for God's sake."

"I thought of that too."

Gari's phone toned again. William picked it up.

"That you?" It was Bud's voice.

"Please say you're not at McDonald."

"'Fraid I can't. May I come see you?"

"Of course."

"If I'm delayed a few minutes, I'll be killing Celia Thompson."

"Could you do it twice?"

At the cabin's small landing target, William and Gari pushed their copter aside to make room for Bud's—which they watched rise from the McDonald lot and flutter toward them across the canyon.

Bud stayed only a few minutes and gave William and Gari very little opportunity to speak. He jumped out of his cab and wrapped his arms around them, embracing them together. "Do you want her?" he asked William.

"Yes, I—"

Bud let out a long breath. "I'm moving out to Delta. I would have wanted to anyway—to have talked Gari into going with me someday. I'll miss both of you... more than I can... I don't even understand why myself. We'll always be a team."

Neither William nor Gari had ever seen Bud cry, and they did not see it now. Somehow the absence of tears made his pain all the more evident.

"There's a caravan going up in three weeks or so," Bud continued; "I'll be with it. That means I'll have just reached L-5 when the alien ship arrives. Let me know if there's anything I can help you with from that perspective."

He backed away from them awkwardly, jumped into his copter, and left.

William and Gari walked slowly back into the house.

"Why," William wanted to know, "did he not ask whether *you* wanted *me?*"

They were back in the bedroom converted into a broadcast studio when she answered:

"Remember that time, eons ago, when we were here, and Bud pushed me into your arms?"

"I'll never forget it. My heart nearly stopped."

"Really?" She was suddenly angry. "You bastard! Then why did it take a year for tonight to happen? Do you have any idea what you put me through? Do you realize what we were doing to poor Bud—for a *year?*"

He shook his head in bewilderment. "But Bud—"

"Is a better person than even *he* thinks he is, better than the world thinks he is—if that's possible. But you're the one who... I mean... don't you see how much alike... no, not how much alike we are but how much our *worlds* are alike? We look out there and see the same things. There's nothing Bud has to offer that can top that—nothing anybody has to offer!"

William, in contrast to Bud, cried easily. Tears were dripping over his happily smiling mouth.

"Bud didn't ask if I wanted you, tonight, because I had already told him. A year ago. Stop that sniveling, damn you, I'm not through being mad yet!" Her eyes were watering too.

"Yes you are. Let's have sex."

"It's a quarter to ten."

He laughed and wiped his eyes. "Okay, make it coffee."

William was ready with his equipment, his notes, and his nerves. A woman with frizzy white hair, from the American Association of Academic Science, was introducing to the television audience the upcoming alien broadcast. She tried to dispel a variety of rumors through stressing our global ignorance.

"... since Dr. Reid discovered how to process the incoming signal in such a way that every frame, not just every thousandth frame, was visible to us. In other words, we have only seen *motion* for twelve days. No pictures from any earlier period have been withheld by any government or private agency.

"So far, every citizen who claims to be able to understand their language by some non-rational means has been exposed as a charlatan or a mental case. It is puzzling, scientists admit, that so little headway has been made in setting up a common language.

"It follows, then, that we have no idea who they are, where they've come from, why they are coming to earth, or even *if* they're coming to earth. We know only that they are alien and that if they choose to take advantage of their opportunity, they can fall easily into an orbit of earth. We know also that, all other things being equal, they should arrive here on March 19th.

"We have heard a speculation that the arriving vessel will pass through L-5, the Lagrangian point number 5, where the Delta Colony is located. This point of gravitational stability is situated on the moon's orbital path and is equidistant from the earth and the moon. L-5 *follows* the moon in its orbit. If there were foundation to this fear, the Delta Colony *would* be in some danger. However, the idea was spread by a simple misprint in Modern Astronomy Magazine. They printed L-5 when they should have printed L-4. L-4 is the corresponding point on the moon's orbit that *precedes* the moon, and it is this point the aliens are expected to pass near. This puts Delta at an even safer distance than the earth itself.

"No, the United States Government is not ignoring the possibility that our visitors might be hostile. I learned today, in fact, that some Congressmen have proposed a retroactive tax to cover a military preparedness venture that is already underway."

Gari chuckled. "I'll bet that's why I haven't heard from Dad lately. He's ranting and filibustering to defeat that tax bill."

At the conclusion of her portion of the broadcast, the woman presented the communications roster: "Tonight we have four segments of eleven minutes each. Dr. Nakayama in Tokyo, Drs. Blythe and Harris in London, Mr. Leon Hillary in Texas, and Drs. Kamlin and Brewster in Melborne."

A commercial followed.

Anger and a feeling of hopelessness collided in William's brain and his ears began to ring. Hillary had taken his time slot! No explanation, no apology, no request. He had simply taken it—somehow.

"You know committees," Gari said gently, "and the way they vote. Maybe they felt obligated because of Hillary's financing here and there. What are you going to do about it, William?"

116

He leaned forward suddenly and began gathering his notes. "Come on," he said, "we're going to the observatory." He shouted into the other bedroom: "Come along, Ganymede, I've got a big fat cowboy for you to chew on!"

Ganymede understood quite a lot just from William's actions and tone of voice; she trotted out ahead of William and Gari and was waiting for them at the copter door.

The clouds were dissipating; Sirius shone through in a small black patch. As the copter lifted off its passengers saw the lights fade out at McDonald and the homes in the valley wink to blackness as the crystals in plastiglass windows switched to opaque. The big telescope dome was opening.

Hillary met them in the copter lot and was infuriatingly generous: he offered William half of his eleven-minute segment. Dubin was apologetically non-commital and accepted the compromise wordlessly.

The crowd of scientists, reporters, government observers and other dignitaries was so large that the gathering had had to assemble in the main telescope housing, which was heated with radiant tubes so the dome could remain open throughout. There was a hope that a picture of the approaching ship might be obtained, even if it showed only a moving point of reflected sunlight.

No parliamentary procedure had been arranged for, and none seemed necessary: there were only whispers prior to the clock's indication of transmission time—at which time even the whispers ceased. If William's deductions proved to be correct, and the augmentations in equipment he ordered had been properly accomplished, this would be the first reception in color. The "snow" on the monitors disappeared abruptly.

Screens—both CRT and liquid crystal—went black. The expected familiar picture of the aliens huddled around an instrument console did not appear.

A floor director spread his palms in an I-don't-know-what's-going-on expression. He contacted his remote video director and then reported: "Nobody else has a picture either, but there's a signal."

On the monitors, a point of white light fell slowly from the top of the picture to the bottom.

"That's a picture of space, I think," William said. He then had to add: "Be quiet please."

The top of the picture began to lighten as if a bright beam were hitting the camera lens. The limb of a planet slipped into view.

"That's not earth!" someone whispered loudly.

"Quiet!" demanded another voice.

"They're showing us their home planet," Hillary said with certainty. "We're not going to talk to them tonight; this is their show."

Suddenly a sound track popped on, as if the projectionist out there had simply failed to engage it to begin with. It was an alien's slow sustained speech—a narration. The words were still unintelligible, but this was the greatest accumulation of them ever transmitted.

The picture zoomed slowly back to show the whole of a gibbous planet . . . water-covered, streaked with clouds, with numerous continents so small they might not have qualified as continents at all. (The press thereafter referred to the place as "the planet of a million islands.")

The picture cut to a view from within the atmosphere, taken by a vehicle moving at incredible speed and exhibiting unheard-of maneuverability. The islands below zipped past. Clouds flashed white, obscured the scene briefly, and suddenly were gone. The water reflected sunlight just like the seas of earth. The narrator might have been pointing out coastlines of interest and speaking of wondrous histories, biologies, technologies—but not a word could be understood.

William licked his lips which had dried from staying open too long. He waited for one thing in particular: he wanted to see their cities.

But there were no cities, and no vehicles, no aircraft, no sign of life except for a handful of aliens in protective suits walking in painful slow motion through lush jungle growths. Red balloons flitted through the air—probably some kinds of gas-filled pollen carriers. Among the trees and plants were flowers and mosses of every imaginable color—there could not have been a fairer test of William's color-reception method—and occasionally there were patches of gray that might have been some kind of mold.

Apparently the aliens had chosen to show a tape from some archeological expedition. But why? It might have had great significance to them—perhaps it was a tape of the discovery of their missing link—but it meant nothing in particular to their earthly audience. Great bones were shown being hoisted out of an excavation.

After the "movie" there was only a minute remaining—during which the scene expected at the opening appeared: aliens huddled together, none of whom spoke. The picture disintegrated. The broadcast was over.

"Waste of time tonight," Gari said to William. "Nakayama's right; they don't know what they're doing."

"I don't think it was a waste of time," said William. "They gave us a long sample of language and pictures of things we can name in English and send back to them. And I think we can prompt them to send us things we're more interested in seeing. I want to see cities, cars, copters, eating utensils, furniture, things like that. Maybe

119

we ought to send them some travelogs—New York City, for instance. And there's something else—just a hunch. I don't think any of that was in slow motion."

Gari started to disagree and then realized: "Only the *people* moved slowly. Those red things zipped around on the wind like dandelion seeds." She had it: "They move at a slower rate than we do!"

"Perhaps they live at a slower rate. Think at a slower rate. *Speak* at a slower rate."

A reporter from Science News was eavesdropping. He asked, "Might they have extremely long life spans then?"

Gari answered excitedly. "That sure would make interstellar travel more practical for them. You can cover a lot of territory if you live for several hundred years!"

William took her arm and steered her out before she and the reporter could do any more speculating. It was already a sure bet that tomorrow's news and next week's magazines would carry fillers on the lives of sea turtles, sloths, lorises and the like.

They looked for Bud in the parking lot. His copter was no longer there.

Chapter 10

Rendezvous

Bud Sullivan knew something William and Gari were learning the hard way: if you're one of the public's playthings, the only way to be left alone is never to hide. At the Delta administration building in the Kennedy Industrial Park of Cape Canaveral, Bud was a famous man but also just an employee—one of the dozen flight-suited men and women having coffee in the executive lounge. No one was trying to find him; billions of people already knew where he was, why he was there, and where he was going—or rather not going. The Delta launch had at the last minute been postponed indefinitely.

A woman—especially attractive, Bud thought, in her silver tight-fitting suit—pushed herself out of a body-formed chair and stepped to the controls of the photogrid across the lounge. "It's not the end of the world," she said. "We'll get there in a few days. How can you people stand not knowing what's happening?"

The grid produced a picture. A bedraggled anchorman—he had apparently been at his post for days—was rambling to fill up time with words to describe no recent developments. "And so, ladies and gentlemen, we have learned that the aliens' additional rocket burn, around 80 hours ago, has indeed insured that the ship's ETA is 3:22 Eastern Time this afternoon; that is, in about an hour and fifteen minutes. We'll have a replay of the photos of their burn, with additional photos taken later showing its enormous spherical shape. Stay tuned for a replay of that tape. For those of you just joining us, we should repeat that the Delta launches scheduled for later today have been postponed due to the unpredictability of the incoming visitors. Not only the Delta launch but several others have been given no-go's...." The anchorman shuffled through his papers to find the list of launch cancellations. "Most interesting among them is the welcome-wagon planned by Hillary and his Alienites. The International Court in The Hague has issued an order restraining Hillary's lift-off of four escort shuttles from the Amon-Carter launch facility in North Texas. Also there's...."

"I'm going for a walk," Bud announced, as he headed for the door.

"Don't you want to get out of that monkey suit?" a friend asked.

Bud grinned. "I'm proud of my monkey suit." He reflexively patted his kangaroo pouch to be sure he wasn't leaving his phone behind.

"We're hopping over to Orlando," said the attractive female, "to kill the evening. Join us?"

"Might," said Bud; "thanks." He thought: Sorry, lady; you're playing it too casual to be for real. That's not the way to get me.

He hopped the tram—hardly more than a moving walkway with shaded chairs—that took him down along Kennedy Parkway to the site of the old Complex 39. In his mind's eye he was superimposing photographs, ghosts, of the famous Vehicle Assembly Building where the first rocket to the moon was built. An obelisk stood there now, which was both a monument to Apollo and a practical structure housing a traffic tower serving the new shuttle runways. Bud imagined himself as Neil Armstrong riding that rickety liquid-fuel bomb that had lumbered up through the clouds and to the moon. People kept making historical comparisons—but it *wasn't* like man's first ride on a steamboat or the flight at Kitty Hawk or even Columbus discovering America.

Who gives a damn about the aliens? Bud mused. What could they possibly have that we haven't got?

Bud did give a damn, however. Like most of the world, he was curious, apprehensive, awed. The aliens had more than likely crossed interstellar space and were alive to tell of it. That alone made them impossible to dismiss. And there were two shiploads of them! Although the second vessel had been "temporarily misplaced," as one commentator had put it, there *was* a second ship.

Bud felt that he was approaching the end of the tramline too soon. He jumped off onto the grass under a warm Florida sun. It was just a mile or so more; he could walk. He surveyed the flatland of Merritt Island and Canaveral, strained to see the towering heavy-launch-vehicle service scaffolds in the hazy distance, scanned the ocean, the cumulus clouds on the horizon, and walked backwards so he could look at the shining structures of the Industrial Park he had left behind him. He was, without quite realizing it, saying goodbye to the sea, the sky, buildings on flat ground, and the signs of progress in space that had

123

bolstered him since childhood. He was bidding the earth farewell.

He would miss Gari. Bud had slept with so many women he would be hard-pressed to supply an approximate count; but Gari thought what she said she thought, felt what she said she felt, wanted what she said she wanted—was who she said she was. Damn her anyway; life was so much easier before. Easier—but smaller.

I wonder whatever happened to Ellen Davis, Bud thought idly, strolling on toward Complex 39. She had been his first lover, when they were 12. He was on the verge of deciding he would miss Ellen Davis when it humorously occurred to him that he was perfectly free to take all his memories with him. They weighed nothing.

The air exploded suddenly with a deafening crack as a shuttle, traveling at just over Mach-I trailed its shock wave over Canaveral. Down the Cape, along the Banana River, banking sharply—a bright point in the sky now— out over the Atlantic. That would be the final NASA maintenance crew returning. The space over earth was cluttered with thousands of working satellites (some dating well back into the 20th Century), but now there were no human beings left up there. The aliens had it all to themselves.

Bud watched the sleek flat ship return at a more respectable speed for its landing. The craft, one of the newer Boeing models, looked amusingly like the old idea of a flying saucer.

"Why are you walking, Bud? They're here!"

"Who?"

"The aliens! Get in."

Bud climbed through the car door his co-worker was holding open. "Let's check out traffic control," said the

124

man as he accelerated toward the tower.

They heard shouting before the elevator reached the top. "Who's controlling the ag-sats? . . . Hit that switch, man, don't ask me why! . . . What's its perigee? . . . God damn, look at that thing travel! . . . What's it going to hit first, the Euro-African weather-eye? . . . Nope, it's after the old 5.6-meter scope; my God, the scope's gone! . . . What's its perigee, damn it? . . ."

Bud watched the displays over the shoulders of the controllers. He suggested: "From the way it's, uh, well look at the velocity, latitude, direction. And here, the apogee potential is changing but . . . aren't they heading for a geosynchronous orbit at around 14,000 kilometers?"

"Jesus, I hope not. That's where most of our hardware is. Hell, if they're not careful, they could wipe out a whole network of communications sats—just mow them down!"

"Oh, I don't know," Bud soothed; "there's a lot of space out there. I'm surprised they managed to bump into the telescope."

The alien ship employed only one burst from its main thrusters but kept its attitude rockets going constantly— for just under an hour—to help break its speed and position it in space. There were no more casualties among robot satellites.

"There she sits," someone said with a shrug, "like Bud said, in geosync orbit over a point off the west coast of South America. Why there, I wonder? A little over a hundred degrees west."

Bud laughed. "Same longitude as McDonald Observatory?"

"I'll check."

Bud was right.

The sun was low over the Florida mainland when Bud stepped out of the tower. He had a fleeting urge to call

William and Gari at McDonald to wish them luck. They, largely, would be taking it from here. But no, calling them was not a good idea. As if aware that Bud's thoughts involved it, the phone in his pouch toned.

"Yes?"

"It's the Canaveral board. I've turned away lots of calls from Leon Hillary, but he insists we let you know he's trying to get to you."

"Okay," Bud said, "tell him you've told me. But I still have nothing to say to him."

Aimlessly, for all intents and purposes, Bud ambled out to the hangars. The three shuttles that would not be taking new residents to Delta were there.

"Hi, Bud." The maintenance engineer did not seem surprised to see astronaut Sullivan poking around the ships.

"Someone told you I was coming?" Bud asked.

"No, should they have? Something I can do for you?"

Bud shook his head and shrugged.

The three white monstrosities seemed to be cowering in the recesses of the hangar as if humiliated by the cancellation of their flight and wishing not to be seen even in the rusty light coming through open 40-meter-high doors. Bud was to have piloted the Goddard. He rested his hand, out of habit, on its body. It was cold. The tanks were full.

The maintenance engineer was watching Bud and pretending not to.

Bud climbed the ladder to get a look into the cockpit, the hatch of which he found unlocked. Inside, on the co-pilot's chair, rested a space helmet and a note. "Bud," said the typewritten message, "Hillary will underwrite the flight."

He probably would, Bud thought. He wondered if the engineer who spied so ineptly had planted the helmet and

126

the challenge. He flicked on the electrical system and watched the banks of instruments come to life. He turned it off again.

Impulsively he pulled out his phone and punched up a long-distance number.

"Mr. Sullivan is out of his office today, in Oklahoma City."

"Would you relay this through to him? This is his son calling."

"Sure thing. How's it going Bud?"

"That you, Gwen? Fine, thanks."

After two more relays, Norman Sullivan, Sr., was on the line. "Thought we said our goodbyes."

"You never watch the news, do you, Dad. Our launch has been postponed."

"All anybody talks about around *here* is little green men from Mars. I'm a little rushed, Bud; what's up?"

"Nothing really; I just felt like calling." The conversation remained at a standstill until Bud said, "I don't want to keep you."

"Son—don't hang up. Just keep the line open. We don't have to say anything. Just don't cut it off."

Bud had carefully avoided suggesting that his Dad might one day visit Delta—Sullivan Sr.'s age and health made that unthinkable. His father had just as carefully, Bud knew, refrained from saying, *Bud, don't go.* It seemed unlikely that the two would ever see each other again.

"I never could keep secrets," the small voice from Bud's phone said. "I transferred a million in credit to Delta for you."

"Dad! I can't—"

"You would have inherited it someday. It doesn't break me. Now don't make me sorry I told you."

"Don't be sorry. I just don't know what to say."

"Good. I love you, son."

While speaking, Bud had sealed the outer lock of the cockpit. After replacing the phone in his pouch he flicked the electrics back on. William would understand this, Bud thought; he always does something extravagant when he's depressed—like buying that dog, getting his hand-tooled engine, trying out the Sledway. . . .

The wheels under the shuttle squeeked as they began to roll. When he was clear of the hangar and heading for the empty runway, Bud called the tower. "I'm going into orbit. I want to see that thing."

"Negative Bud, that's absolutely a no-go!"

"I know, but I'm doing it anyway. Thought you might like to know."

"No—you don't understand! They're—"

Bud switched the tower off. What he didn't hear couldn't hurt him, not today.

Bud considered the aliens:

Bunch of showoffs. Think you're really hot with your Buck Rogers atomics. Well, get a load of what a simple chemical reaction can do. And a good old IBM computer!

Atmospheric jets whining up to speed as the shuttle poised on the runway, Bud typed in orbital coordinates (if he had been setting a course for the moon, Delta, or any of a number of major robot satellites, the punch of a single button would have sufficed).

He engaged the AAM—automatic avoidance mechanism—which would steer him clear of any orbiting equipment, each piece of which emitted a location beacon. As he did so, myriad lights popped on at the consoles of air and space controllers all over the world. There simply was no safe way to sneak into space.

While attaching his air hose, Bud watched scattered

128

signals before him turn from red to green. As the last one greened, the ship (Bud was merely a passenger now) leapt ahead as if shot from a catapult. The shuttle screamed back toward Complex 39; the control tower sank rapidly as he zoomed past; the line of Kennedy Parkway wiped across his field of vision as he banked; looking back he saw the structures of Industrial Park tilt up and peel away; he jetted out over the Atlantic, eastward, toward the night.

The shuttle climbed to 22,000 meters and then, at roughly Mach-IV, used a solid wall of air to send it nosing straight up. Boosters cut in and slammed Bud back into his seat cushion. He laughed raucously at the sensual thrill of it and emitted the college "Ya-hooo!" which had become one of his trademarks with the press and the public. A rocket jockey indeed he was.

No one heard him this time. Insanely though, the alert-light on his radio was flickering: someone was calling. "Not now, you idiots!" he yelled at the deaf radio.

He tipped forward again, out of his perpendicular climb, and the ship was slowly rolled so that in orbit his cab would face earthward. Below were lights on the African coast; Bud could pick out Villa Cisneros directly below, Dakar to the south and Casablanca to the far north. The boring blackness of the Sahara was relieved by something he had seen only once before: tiny circles of glowing yellow—brush fires lighted by farmers clearing the land for pre-rainy-season planting. The earth seemed to be spinning more slowly when tomorrow began to brighten the blue curve of the earth, and the sun moved out of eclipse. The terminator split New Guinea in half.

On his pass through 100° west longitude, Bud reoriented the craft to allow him to see outward; he saw only stars, one of which was probably his quarry.

129

The sun was about to disappear again when Bud saw that the earth stood still beneath him. Twilight was arriving at the mouth of the Amazon; in less than an hour it would arrive at Cape Canaveral. Rookie astronauts were forever becoming disoriented by the illusion Bud next chuckled through: with the shuttle's engines pounding as powerfully as before, aiming him toward the east, the earth was in retrograde; he seemed to be slipping backward, back across Brazil, Colombia, the Galapagos—back to 100° west. The feeling the sight produced was one of falling; whereas the ship was in reality rising, maneuvering toward a geosynchronous point along an imaginary equator high over the surface of the earth.

Bud could see the alien ship: a tiny crescent moon.

The phone box on his belly toned. This was such an obvious but unheard-of and creative method of communication that Bud felt obliged to answer it. He realized that the phone transmission had only about a hundred kilometers of air to wade through to reach him, and he wondered why no one had tried such a thing before. Just tradition, probably—phones are for earth, radios are for air and space. Bud answered, "Hello, Outer Space; whom shall I say is calling?"

The laughter was instantly recognizable. "It's William, Captain Courageous. Don't talk, just listen. Start imaging on the aliens at once; give us two-camera, wide and close-up, coverage." Bud adjusted the controls that carried out William's order. "Good, we're getting it. Turn your geiger counter on *and leave it on*! Move in as close as it seems safe to do, and not a centimeter closer. Give us a commentary of what you see. When you turn on your ship's radio, the President will order you to return to Delta Base immediately. Don't do anything stupid. Do what you're told. I just want to see as much as you can show us before you have to turn around. You're getting pretty close. Better turn on your radio. Gari and I are at McDonald, incidentally. Hillary's here too, sneaking around with Dubin working up a conspiracy to do God knows what. Good luck—and don't take your eyes off that geiger counter!"

The President—whom Bud had met on numerous occasions and knew as "Stevie"—spoke with uncharacteristically measured words, clearly trying to impart some meaning without spelling it out for general consumption. "Mr. Sullivan, if you do exactly as instructed you will be pardoned from court-martial proceedings." Okay, Bud translated, they're seeing this as a military operation, and I'm in the way. "Make a hasty reconnaissance, never approaching too close, and then return to base as quickly as possible." They can't see enough detail through their telescopes and—good grief, the military's going to blow it up! "You have almost 35 minutes." They're not quite ready with their missiles. "Do you understand me?"

"Thoroughly, Mr. President. I'm switching off the guidance system temporarily so that I can move around the thing. It's perfectly spherical—looks like a basketball, seams and all. It's . . . 303.66 meters in diameter, and—"

The phone toned again. "William?"

"Me again. Does it have any windows, ports?"

"Not that I can see. I'm moving in a little closer."

"Antennae?"

"I think so. I see some instruments sticking out of a hole; and there's another batch of them."

The President's voice came from the radio: "You are alone aren't you, Bud?"

"I'm alone - speaking to Dr. Reid by phone."

131

"Phone?"

William continued to prompt: "Any activity, anything moving?"

"No. Listen, William, why are they setting up to—"

"Possible contamination. Would you believe that it only recently occurred to anybody that a decontamination and debriefing facility would be needed in case they land? It's not ready yet."

"Well, why not meet them up here? Move a space station into place and meet them in the most sterile environment possible: space."

"I heard that suggestion, Bud," the President said; "it's a good one, and I just put it under advisement."

Suddenly phone and radio alike carried a high-pitched static wail.

"What the hell is that?" Bud yelled.

He could barely make out William's reply; it sounded like: "Hillary's sending them a message or signal of some kind."

"Get him to cut it out! Somebody ought to have that guy arrested!"

The wailing stopped as abruptly as it had started.

"Bud—come back down," William ordered.

"I want to get you a close-up on those instrument pods. I can see some movement at one of them. Looks like an optical instrument of some kind. Bet it's a TV camera."

"How about radiation?" William asked.

"Negligible. No, wait, I'm picking up a little more from this side. I must be approaching the business end of the thing. Yep, there's a big round hole."

"Anything that looks like armaments?" the President asked.

"Not that I can see, but everything about this ship looks retractable. Hey—something's happening. A thing is coming out of that hole. And the instrument pods are retracting."

"Get out of there!" William insisted.

"I think you're right," said Bud.

The thing coming out of the hole looked like a propulsion nozzle. "Oh my God," Bud whispered when he saw it begin to glow. He dove frantically to his controls to set the sequence that would blast him away—afraid he had acted too late. The nozzle's glow was already too bright to look at directly through his viewports. The geiger digital flickered violently at its highest setting and then broke.

Bud screamed to the world, "Aw shit!" as he deduced that he was a dead man.

The sun exploded.

Chapter 11

Eyewitness

Daren Cole cried out in horror. His mother looked in to see what had prompted his outburst. Daren had not made a sound in months. Childish rebellion, his mother assumed; trying to scare us into thinking he's possessed so he can get out of work. A worthless, useless 12-year-old sponge. And there he was again watching the damn TV. Taking it seriously like some driveling baby, his eyes bugged out as if he'd seen the devil himself. Mrs. Cole snapped off the set; it's faded sepia picture crumpled and was sucked out through a point of light (the set was more than 50 years old).

"It's nearly night and you haven't done a lick of work," she said, not in anger but merely as an observation and to have something to say.

Daren switched the set back on. He acted as if his mother were not in the room, were not in existence—as if the set had accidentally turned itself off.

"... instruments aboard are responding for the most part," an announcer was saying excitedly, "but Bud doesn't answer his radio." The picture was a wavering earth-originated telescopic shot of the shuttle flopping crazily end over end against a field of black. "The alien ship is continuing its blast—which can be seen by much of this hemisphere as a bright star, even in daylight. The burn accelerates the ship westward, which almost surely indicates an intention to enter the atmosphere...."

Daren ran outside. Men and boys on the plateau beneath him were hurrying to finish planting before nightfall. Rain was predicted, and for this crop of wild wheat it was now or never. Out beyond the mesas and pinnacles sunlight still edged crowds of saguaro cactus—their arms raised and frozen like a praying multitude. There would be no sunset color in the cloudless sky.

There, just as the announcer had predicted, high and to the southwest: the brightest star there ever was.

Why isn't it moving? Daren wondered. Its rockets ought to be pushing it faster than the eye can follow. The TV'll tell me.

"Air and space traffic has been alerted," the announcer told Daren in the apartment, "and it is expected that the military will make some move to warn them not to land until preparations have been completed. We can now take you to outer space, to OO-IX's picture of the alien vessel...." In this picture, Daren was amazed to see, the ship was moving away from the camera at phenomenal speed!

Daren heard his mother's skirt rustle and knew she was standing behind him as he sat watching his electronic wizard, his teacher, his proof that there was an outside world.

"I'm not going to let your father catch you like this,"

she said as if she were talking uselessly to a blind deaf mute. "It's bad enough that you didn't work in the field today. It would kill him to come home and find you playing with your toys."

Daren thought: But don't you understand what's happening?

Once again she turned off the set.

Apparently unperturbed, Daren leaned over till he was lying on the floor and tugged a crate out from under his bed. He took from it a flat disc no bigger than a coin, slipped it into the pocket of his too-large plaid shirt, and left.

He climbed the bouldered rim to the top of the mesa inside which his community dwelled like the Pueblo Indians of centuries ago. The point of bright light had moved somewhat to the west as if following the sun. The sky was darker; twilight would be swift. Lights had come on along the Arizona Sledway far to the south. Daren had made pilgrimages to the recently constructed Sledway. He always found it too quiet to be so powerful; it only produced whooshes of wind as each car sledded by. His people had no interest in the Sledway; to them it was already just another feature of the desert, just there.

The coin-shaped object was a radio. Several men had hijacked a rickety old truck, and there had been a carton of them in the back. Daren sat cross-legged in a pocket formed by mesquites that grew around a slab of rock. He squeezed the electricity-producing ring around the radio, laid it on a stone beside him, and waited for it to tell him the latest news.

Daren was second-generation in the community; most of the youngsters were third. They called themselves the people. Others, in cities and civilized countrysides, called them hill people. There were other such groups; whether they lived in hills, swamps, mountains, deserts, forests or abandoned areas of towns, they were called hill people. They were so ignored that not even census takers could estimate their total number.

Many hill communities had sprung up in the late 20th Century when taxes had reached a long-predicted intolerable rate. Families and individuals just wandered off undramatically leaving no forwarding addresses. They set up hidden towns—some of them communal, some individualistic, some of them law-abiding, some criminal. Some of them survived, some did not.

A second wave of drifters led to a bolstering, in size at least, of many of the camps. Overreacting to the untenable tax burden, a vote-conscious Congress obliterated, with the fall of a single Constitutional axe, the so-called welfare system that had taken taxes to guarantee an "income" to the unemployed, "compensation" for unsupported children, "insurance" against unprepared-for old age, and apartments for the "deserving poor." Led in good faith for their whole lifetimes to expect never-ending governmental succor, some of the low-income and no-income citizens—those who did not turn to crime or commit suicide—became gypsies. A good many gypsies ultimately found homes among the hill people. One such was Daren's father, Bill Cole, a migrant farm laborer out of work for a decade because there were no more un-automated farms.

There was only the faint light of the cliff-dwelling reflected off the side of Man Mountain. The moon, Daren knew, would rise much later as a fat crescent. The alien's torch had set with the sun. The radio provided more data than Daren could deal with, but he understood essentially what was going on. "In the atmosphere," a newsman said, "the thing acts just like a rock with a rocket; there's nothing aerodynamic about the design of it. Scientists speculate that its unusual stability must be due to tremendous gyroscopic forces within. The ship slipped gently into the air with a constantly burning engine, making an almost straight-down descent veering only a little westward and northward from the original latitude and longitude. This would be a prohibitively expensive trick for our ships to pull off. It's out over the Pacific now, and people in Hawaii are watching it fall toward their eastern horizon. I have a bulletin here on the situation with Bud Sullivan. His ship is in a temporarily safe orbit; he still seems to be unconscious; and a rescue shuttle is being readied at Canaveral to go up and bring him down."

Another announcer's voice came on and talked about missiles with low-yield atomic warheads being launched from an Hawaiian base. "We're observing radar and an image produced by an infra-red detector in orbit. We're looking at a screen with one big dot and three little ones, the missiles. The missiles are gaining very slowly because the speed of the alien craft is almost sufficient to outrun them. The missiles are on target ... no ... they're moving aside, being shunted by some kind of force. One just impacted on the ocean and exploded. God only knows where the other two are going. Wait ... they have been blown up harmlessly by ground controllers, apparently."

The first announcer's voice came back: "The ship made a sweeping turn—it's now at an altitude of about 22,000 meters—and is descending toward the California coast."

Daren tried another station. "... are warned to stay indoors," a rather hysterical man was shouting. "That's all along the coast but particularly around Santa Barbara. The engine seems to be fairly fall-out free, but the sheer heat and direct radiation are staggering—and very very dangerous. The ship is behaving like ... like a curve ball, almost zig-zagging, so it is impossible to say just what its route and destination are. Some say McDonald Observatory."

"That's right, Ken," a woman's voice interjected, "in fact the people at McDonald are packing up to make a fast getaway or at least move to a safe distance. The way things look now, they'll have less than an hour to evacuate. Let's see what's happening in California. Are you there, Pete Johnson?"

"Yes, Cynthia, we're here at Mount Wilson hoping to catch a glimpse . . . Jesus!"

"We saw it on the monitor here, Pete—"

"But it was the *way* it happened. It looked like the monster came right out of the sun, which is orange and is about to touch the Pacific horizon. Like a piece of the sun split off, came at us, then shot off to the east. And hear that? Like rolling thunder that just won't quit!"

"Any danger from radiation, Pete?"

"None that I've heard about so far."

Daren leapt to his feet. East! It's coming this way!

"Ladies and gentlemen," announcer Ken said, "we have just spoken to Leon Hillary, who does think McDonald is the aliens' destination because, he says, 'They know this is where their friends are.' He says advanced races with such awesome capabilities would not attempt a landing unless they already had solved any decontamination problem. He's not sure, however, how a machine the size of a small moon will be able to land in the Davis Mountains. He says Drs. Reid, Copalin, Dubin and some others have already, as he put it, 'abandoned ship,' and he himself has a copter waiting just in case. . . ."

Before Daren caught his first glimpse of the ship, his mind had reached a non-verbal conclusion: he would never go back home, except maybe to pick up a jacket and some food. Why this event should have determined his future he could not have said. But the people, his people, were already an unimportant memory.

A brilliant ball of light popped out of a glow that had blossomed over a mountain to the southwest. As it traversed the southern horizon long shadows, from tall cactus and pinnacles of rock, fanned out and made wheeling spokes on the desert floor. The effect was dizzying and, Daren surmised, was a sight no man had seen before. An atmospheric halo, like a ring around the moon, followed the pseudo-sun over the eastern edge of the world.

"... still losing altitude over New Mexico...."

"... too low to be a safe target for any weapon capable of damaging it...."

"... over the Texas/New Mexico border...."

"... entering the Davis Mountains. The thing is obviously spinning wildly. It's rocket has been extinguished and the nozzle is retracted. Tiny fins apparently give it lift as it spins. Oh—oh—the spin has stopped and the rocket has started up again, sending the ship upward, and it's—it's—I can only describe it as *peeling*, like an orange. Pieces of the spherical shell are coming down. Oh, of course, they're landing legs! It's very near the observatory. We have, I'm told, a picture from the McDonald facility. A camera crew still on the scene reports that the roar is deafening and trees are breaking up due to pressure from the thing. Oh my God! It's coming down right on top of the huge Harvard-Hillary radio dish! Look at that! Any of you only hearing this on radio are being cheated of the most phenomenal photos I've ever seen. The dish is melting, cracking, curling up at the rim. There went one of the smaller domes at McDonald—just sailing through the air! There couldn't be a single home left intact in that valley. We've lost our picture and sound from McDonald. What you see now is being taken from a copter a good 20 kilometers away. Let's talk to the copter."

"Hello, John Soares in that copter you just mentioned, pulling back even farther because it looks like the thing is increasing its thrust for some reason. The copter—I don't know if you can hear it or not—is rattling from the continuous shock waves. We're going to have to sit down or fall down. The ship is rising again! We can't see the vessel at all now, just a ball of fire that's getting bigger— just like a balloon being blown up. It's above Mount Locke, and I can see by the light of it that there's simply nothing left of McDonald. The thing seems to be heading back west. The Davis Mountains all around us are burning, sending up so much smoke that we can't even see the fireball anymore...."

"...an arc, like it's taking a giant step over the state of New Mexico...."

"...perhaps looking for a clearer landing site, the Arizona desert...."

It was much too early for dawn and the light was rising in the wrong place for the moon. Daren scrambled from his mesa-top perch, down the rim of boulders and into the mouth of the cliff slot that had been cut by nature, Indians, and modern man; and up to his fourth-story dwelling. His father was on the couch dozing with a glass of liquor on the floor by his hand. Daren grabbed a jacket and charged into the kitchen where his mother was lazily loading a dented old clothes-washing machine. "*Now* you feel like going outside," she grumbled. Daren took several lumps of cold bread (she did not object, just shook her head in helplessness); he looked up at her and thought: Come with me! A spaceship is going to land someplace

141

close and if you don't run you're going to die! But he knew what her reply would be; so no words came out. Before he ran from the kitchen he thought, experiencing fear and terrible sadness: Goodbye, Mother. "Sounds like thunder," she said, looking up; but the prospect of rain did not interest her much either.

The world was lighted as if by a wandering full moon. A wind rustled the creosotebush, mesquites and ironwood. Yellow blooms were flying from whipped palo verde trees and tumbleweed were taking to the air. Shadows on the ground were turning again, and this time Daren was inside the spokes of the ghostly wheel. He climbed. He did not look up. On the back side of the people's mountain Daren stopped, awestruck, to look northward where the shadow of his mountain was crawling out across the desert like an arm reaching to infinity. A boiling cloud of sand carried light with it through the passes on either side of the mountain. Daren was afraid the sand might burn him and the thunder might make him deaf. He squirmed through a split in a boulder which led to his private discovery: a coal-black tunnel that went down into the heart of the mountain.

The earth vibrated; rocks and dirt fell on him. He looked up quickly before descending into the cave. Even the sky was on fire.

His radio, its voices coming muffled from his pocket, talked about touchdown in an uninhabited mountain-desert area in Arizona. Just before he had crawled too deeply into the mountain for the radio waves to reach him, he heard:

"Traffic was halted on the Arizona Sledway, but not before..."

As if stressing Daren's terrifying solitude, the radio's

142

voice faded with the light as he slipped lower down the vibrating stone passageway.

From TV adventures and educational programs Daren understood a thing or two about radioactivity. He knew it was invisible, like X-rays, and people could die from it; it was in the air and on things you touch. It eventually went away but, he dimly remembered, under some conditions it might take millions of years. But he put that possibility out of his mind, just as he avoided thinking about scorpions, centipedes, rattlers and no telling what else that might be there in the dark with him. He reasoned he would be safer from both vermin and poisonous air the deeper he could go.

He had never been as frightened as he was in the first few hours. He heard a drip but could not think of a safe way to explore for water and still be sure of finding his way back to the tunnel that could take him out again; his throat was so dry it hurt. He imagined being lost forever trying to find his way in the dark. He imagined that the mouth of the tunnel had been sealed by falling boulders. He imagined himself starving to death, running out of air, watching his skin decay and fall off until his eyes plopped out of their sockets. He imagined the cockeyed view from two disembodied eyes looking up from where they had rolled on the cavern floor. He pictured a heap of ashes that had once been his cliffside home and saw the people he knew crumbling to dust in a smoldering gray dune.

He fared better later. He occupied himself by throwing flint pebbles against the stone of the cavern walls and watching the sparks that made tracings in the air which looked like tree twigs. He explored around the mouth of his exit route with his hands, "seeing" the contours in his mind. He made one ritual of eating the bread and another of trying to estimate the passage of time. He continued to resist the dangerous urge: to seek out that water, which constantly dripped.

Hungry, dehydrated, still frightened, he finally determined that he might as well go out—maybe the radiation was gone—rather than die in this tomb. His computations told him he had been buried, sightless, for three nights and two days. He suspected he would find dawn breaking on the outside.

The debris in front of his exit was fairly easily shoved aside. It was daylight all right, a very bright afternoon (his figures had been about 14 hours on the long side). The shadows of the peaks, hills and pinnacles surrounding the arroyo were all wrong: their crests had been shaved off, smoothed. The spindly pinnacle whose shadow, cast at midnight by a full moon, used to point almost directly to the north star—it wasn't there at all anymore. A million years of erosion had happened here a couple of days ago.

There was a gentle hot breeze, as there was on most spring afternoons, but no birds sang. Instead there were remote human voices. And more than one copter's rotors disturbed the air somewhere near; Daren saw a big one of the type used to carry 200 or more passengers to and from intercontinental airports. It seemed to be flying low to stay in the protection of Twin Peaks, and it seemed to be shying clear of a glittering path that fanned out on the floor between mountains. It wasn't water; it was like splashes of glass.

Daren looked at the shadow of Twin Peaks closely for the first time: the two mounds he had always thought of as breasts had lost both nipples. He laughed. Everything was going to be all right—as long as there was something funny in the world.

The copter landed out of sight. Daren made his way around the mountain ledge to see what more there was to be seen. There were two encampments: one snug against Twin Peaks—with prefab houses and many little personal copters—and another farther out on the desert floor consisting of rows of tents and prefabs with lots of people wandering about. That's where the big copter had landed; from it were streaming more people. Another copter was coming in—a sky hook that trailed a heavy-looking brown machine on its cables. It occurred to Daren to turn on his radio.

The first two stations were playing music; the third had a baseball game; on the fourth, a newscaster was saying:

". . . act as if they're still in outer space. They come to their cameras, try to speak to us in that sluggish drawl of theirs, show us some pretty pictures, and then listen and watch as our scientists do essentially the same thing to them. Dr. Reid has asked all parties vying for time to allow him three uninterrupted days for an extensive experiment. He seems to have general agreement except from Leon T. Hillary, still recovering at Baylor Hospital in Dallas, who keeps insisting that the aliens will talk freely when they're good and ready. Hillary's camp at the landing site continues to grow, incidentally; and the whereabouts of the second alien ship is still unknown. On other newsfronts... In Capetown today, President Ndaba, in a dramatic and surprising speech to United Nations visitors, broke South Africa's remaining ties with the Chinese Communists. This came hot on the heels of. . . ."

Daren selected another station.

". . . that the Starprobe Project might now fall under the very military classification which previously had no funds for it. Senator Copalin of New York says he will fight this now as he fought it before. The weather scene—flash flood warnings have been issued for parts of Southern Arizona...."

The otherwise clear sky did have dark clouds lying on the northern horizon. Daren switched off the radio and turned his attention to the camp at the base of Twin Peaks. He had to get over there somehow, across that dry radioactive river bed. He wanted a good look at the alien sphere almost as badly as he wanted food.

For the moment, juicy pads of prickly-pear cactus were all around. He would not starve.

Part III

LOOKING DOWN

Chapter 12

Lessons

Jeno-Hald held a saturated towel against Eroi's forehead; some of the liquid trickled around his ears and dripped onto the hospital bed. When Eroi reached up to keep a rivulet of alcohol out of his eyes, Jeno took his hand and held it.

"Did you know," Jeno asked gently, "that this system has a planet with a ring so dense it looks like a solid disc? It's number six. Our scope is on the fourth planet now; we're coming pretty close to it; you ought to—"

"What happened to me?" Eroi asked, wanting only to have his suspicions confirmed.

"You fainted. I think it's time."

Eroi nodded. "I had my first pain several days ago."

"Why didn't you tell?"

"If—if we had a doctor . . . can't you find the medicine?"

"I've looked. Everybody's looked. We don't know for

certain which is the right one or how much to give. Don't worry. People used to go through this without pain-killers all the time. Nobody ever died from becoming a man."

"It's not pain that frightens me."

"Nobody ever died from becoming a woman either."

"Would you want me for a wife?"

"Of course."

Eroi pulled his hand away from Jeno's. "Tell me Jeno," he sneared; "would *you* want to be *my* wife?"

Jeno did not know how to answer that. He understood Eroi's plight and could easily exchange points of view with him. Jeno and Eroi had been closest of childhood friends—Jeno the child of the President, Eroi the child of the chief communications officer—privileged, educated beyond their ages, inseparable co-conspirators in mischief, incorrigible to the adults, leaders to the children. They had made a religion of a single assumption: that when the time came, both would be men, and they would share a wife. The three of them would ultimately rule the traveling world when Hald and Rool were too old to continue at their demanding posts.

Luckily Jeno did not have to answer Eroi's question. The ailing youth's anxiety got the better of him and he lost consciousness.

Jeno began preparing himself: Eroi probably *was* going to be a woman. By now Eroi could probably feel things, faintly perhaps, but feel them nevertheless, that weren't right under his shell. Jeno suspected that Eroi had lost hope—with reason.

"How is he?" Pata-Hald, Jeno's younger sibling asked; he was leaning against the frame of the infirmary door. "Or should I get used to using feminine designations? What's the situation?"

148

"It's too soon to know," Jeno lied a little. "What are you doing here?"

"The other children sent me. Unanimous vote. They want to know." Maliciously, the little creature sing-songed: "If you don't tell me, we'll all come in here and sit on the floor till he—or she—comes out."

Jeno was angry, but he had learned that it could be disastrous for a leader to express emotion; it betrayed personal involvement. "Tell them I'll come talk to them. Now get out."

Pata did not budge.

"Eroi will be in great pain tonight," Jeno said, "and he will not want an audience for it—not even me. Why does his gender matter so much to the children?"

"We want to know whether we have two leaders like before, or just one."

It was reasonable curiosity, but for some reason Pata's naming it was the most infuriating thing yet. "Get out," Jeno said sharply letting his level-headedness slip.

Pata smiled accusingly and left.

Jeno made sure the basin was filled with plenty of towels and that they were easily within Eroi's reach, then he too left the room and pulled the door quietly shut behind him.

Eroi's mind was swirling in his half-sleep. We're all going to die, he thought unemotionally, so what does anything matter? Himi's ship will find and destroy us, or the gray stuff will get into the nucleusphere eventually, or we will crash trying to land. If I'm a woman, I'll ask for death a little early, that's all. Jeno will look at me with tenderness and protectiveness... I'd rather die!

Death was no longer mysterious. They had learned to live with the threat of it. Eroi remembered when he had

149

committed murder, treason, and mutiny in a single act; for a mere child it had been a phenomenal accomplishment. Eroi remembered....

Hald and his wife and co-husband were trailing the procession of adults into the air-tunnel—a mass-transit device that could take a hundred or more through the vacuum of the innersphere without space suits. Behind the adults, Jeno was bringing up the rear, herding the children from the nursery before him. Eroi was in the middle of that children's death march. The spheres were stopped; there was no gravity. Once all were in the tunnel, it would close, disengage, and float—pulled by cables—to a lock of the outersphere. Jeno and Eroi were dripping oils of anxiety, but the adults thought nothing of it. No one had discovered the youths' plan; no one would have believed it possible if they had.

Jeno had arranged to be the one to deliver death-pills to the nursery; he had administered them to some of the children but not to all. To others—carefully selected for supposed intelligence and maturity—he had given sedatives of the sort often administered prior to an acceleration. He and Eroi had taken stimulants. The condemned children were placed in line ahead of Eroi; the merely sedated ones were between Eroi and Jeno at the end of the line.

"Go ahead, Father," Jeno called out in a very shakey voice; "we're following you."

When Eroi reached the air lock, he slammed it shut while Jeno sequenced the departure of the air-tunnel at a panel beside him on the wall. Before he lost consciousness, Eroi saw Jeno frantically pulling his way weightlessly, back to the command center to reverse the self-destruct mechanism.

150

They were murderers. But what did death matter now? What did anything matter?

Eroi refused to emerge from the infirmary. The children laughed when they heard it.

"She can tell us stories," Pata said, giggling.

"She can prepare our meals; she'll be much better at it now than she used to be," Zeno smirked.

"Aw—she'll make us pick up our toys!" said Zena, Zeno's twin.

Jeno frowned and raised his hand to shut them up. He had a control over them that the adults used to consider magical. "I'm not sure about any of that," he said, thoughtfully. "But you have no right to be cruel to her. Statistically, one out of three of you will be female. Theoretically, every one of you could be." He thought for a moment and then announced: "For now, Eroi is still second in command, just like she used to be."

There was general laughter until the children realized he was serious.

"I won't take work orders from a woman," Pata said flatly.

The others seemed to agree with him.

"Yes you will. All of you will," said Jeno.

That night, after the others were asleep, Jeno took a section of pipe and demolished the door to the infirmary.

Eroi lay on the slab of a bed in the center arms hanging limp off the sides, head turned in what would be an uncomfortable position, eyes shut. Her body was caked with coagulated fluid, and pieces of shell were scattered everywhere. The stench was awful; Jeno assumed she was dead.

The medicine chests had been dumped empty; one of them had been ripped off the wall. Jeno had cautiously taken away anything marked lethal, but there was no way to guess what combinations of the remaining chemicals might do.

Eroi was alive, barely. Jeno found the bottles she must have emptied into her stomach, but their labels meant nothing to him. All he could think of to do was wait. He cleaned away and incinerated the pieces of shell, wiped her body clean with alcohol, covered her lightly with a soft cloth (he remembered vividly how sensitive new skin was; his was only now achieving some toughness), and, when she began to stir, forced her to drink a few drops of water.

"I can't stand your looking at me," was the first thing she said.

He pulled a screen between himself and the bed. He waited for her to speak again.

"I can't be your wife," she said, clearing phlegm from her throat.

He waited for more.

"I'll be useless, so I want to die."

"What else are you thinking?" he asked, trying not to be consoling in his tone of voice.

"It's like—suddenly becoming wise."

"Really? What do you mean?"

"I see things now. I know why they keep children uneducated until after metamorphosis. I know why they have all these myths about how special women are. We should have trusted them and kept ourselves stupid."

Jeno was smiling. "You call that wisdom? Remember the 'they' you mention don't exist anymore. There's just us. Keep thinking."

"How does my voice sound?"

152

"It sounds the same to me. But it will change, you know."

"The children will accept me if I go to the nursery and do what's expected of me—isn't that right?"

"That's right."

She said, after a long silence, "Leave me alone."

Jeno rose without another word and left.

"All right, men," said Jeno, making sure he was clearly heard even to the opposite side of the nucleusphere. "This drill is partly simulated, partly real. I don't want any of you to make reference to tapes or books or notes. But do all the computation you need at the calculators, pads and pens set out for you." Someone snickered, probably at being called a man.

"In order to make our course-corrective burn that will take us to planet three, first we have to stop the revolution of the spheres. I know it'll take a while to get them going again, and this means we'll be weightless, well, for a day or two, I think. But this time, I want to actually lock the ship into position for a burn. Is everyone here?"

"Eroi's not. She's in the recording room. Sulking," said Pata, who was ready to assist Jeno at the pilot console.

"Mimo," Jeno yelled, "get on the intercom and warn Eroi that she should tie herself down." He faced the twins at the inner-ship-systems console who were wide-eyed and open-mouthed in anticipation. "Okay, Zeno and Zena, it's all yours. Stop the spheres. And take your time!" To Sanz, at the video board, Jeno said, "Give us a starfield on the masterscope; I have no idea how to read some of these displays so we'd better be able to see with our eyes whether we're stable or not. Dell—are you standing by on propulsion? We'll need actual power on the attitude nozzles."

Dell was directly over Jeno's head. "It's all set to go,"

he said; "my finger's right over the button."

Jeno's voice dropped to a whisper (he hoped awareness of his ignorance could be limited to only a few,) and he spoke to Pata, who was strumming his fingers on the computer keyboard impatiently. "First, type in the word 'simulation,' and ask the display for a functional definition."

Pata did so. The writing on the tube confirmed that by calling for a simulation, the operator's instructions would be carried out only computationally, not in fact. The engine was not going to accidentally start up. "Okay, Pata, type in 'simulation'—and don't misspell it! Now enter these coordinates." Jeno tossed a sheet of paper under little Pata's nose, "And see if they agree with the data bank's idea of where the third planet is located relative to our present position. Okay, now ask for a read-out of our present speed and trajectory."

"Hey Jeno, nothing's happening," the twins yelled together.

Pata suggested: "Maybe the computer can handle only one system at a time. Want me to turn it off here?"

"I—I guess so. Instruct it to hold all that in memory first."

When Pata waved that this had been accomplished, one of the twins said, "Still nothing happening."

"I'd better go have a look," Jeno told Pata as he unfastened his safety belt.

Then it happened. There was a chilling sound of cables straining and heavy metal being twisted; then the floor was yanked out from under Jeno. The picture of stars on the masterscope began to turn. "The attitude jets!" Jeno screamed, "cut them in now, fast!" He tried to grab a protrusion (made actually for this purpose) on a console; he missed. He slid off the equitorial band and tumbled

154

toward the machinery in the hub opposite the masterscope.

"My chair is tilting automatically!" Taxa screamed.

"I'm getting sick!" said Oiro.

"Look at Jeno!" Hina cried hysterically. "He's hurt!"

Jeno screamed back: "I'm all right." He was hanging on a catwalk. "Shut off the masterscope, Sanz." It was making Jeno and everyone looking at it dizzy.

"Hey, quiet everybody." Pata called for attention and got it fairly promptly since he seemed to know something the others did not. "Here's the situation; it says here we should have started the attitude jets *before* stopping the spheres. The outer shell has to be stopped first; it just drifts when the turning spheres are in free descent."

Jeno laughed nervously. "You cheated. I said no books. But thanks. Does it say what we do to correct the problem."

"Not a word."

Jeno asked Sanz to switch the masterscope back on. The universe was turning more slowly. "I guess we fixed it," Jeno muttered to himself; but he wondered whether burning the attitude jets for too long could shove the ship off course.

"Jeno, Hina and Oiro fainted, " Taxa reported.

"I don't blame them," Jeno said. "Anybody else?"

"No," said a number of children proudly.

"Good."

"Jeno, what's that bright star over there?" Dell asked.

"The fourth planet."

"May I try to get a close-up of it?"

Jeno laughed. "Not now!"

At last the constant hum of the nucleusphere was stilled. Their chairs had sent out arm and leg pads to become acceleration couches, all facing the masterscope.

It had taken longer than even Jeno had predicted, but finally they were weightless.

Jeno, still clinging to the catwalk behind them, floated free with a kick that sent him toward his crew at the equitorial band. The masterscope's picture was front-projected; the children watched Jeno's swimming shadow eclipse the stars on the huge round screen as he returned to them.

Once more strapped in beside Pata, Jeno instructed, "Now let's do the simulated burn."

Pata swallowed hard, hoping he had not made an error in programming, and pressed the activate button. The video displays before him immediately danced with figures and diagrams, but there was no accelerating explosion. The display information said that if they had made that particular burn, they would have attained a cometary orbit around the sun and ultimately would have been incinerated within it. Jeno did not announce the results publicly. "Now ask the computer to try that same burn all along our trajectory. I'd like to know where it would have worked."

Pata laboriously typed in the request. The answer: nowhere.

"Jeno?" It was Eroi's voice coming from Jeno's intercom.

"I hope you've been paying attention to all of this," he said to her.

"See if we have *passed* the point?" she suggested. "Ask the computer to try that exact burn over the space we've already covered."

Pata tried it. The results were negative.

"Does that mean we're going in the wrong direction?" Eroi asked."

"Not necessarily," Jeno answered, frustrated.

After instructing the twins to cheat and find all the information they could on how to re-start the spheres, he said to Pata, "We'll keep trying till we get it."

"Yes, master," Pata said sarcastically.

Jeno was exhausted. His long alcohol bath had helped, but he still did not feel like sleeping. His cabin lights were still on. He lay naked and sensually aware of his inert young body. His hands explored newly exposed muscles and skin so sensitive he could feel differences in air temperature. He felt many things no hard-shelled child ever dreamed of.

The three children in the next room were quarreling, shouting about something. Jeno clanged on the wall with the closest thing at hand, a belt buckle, and shouted, "Go to sleep in there."

The noise stopped. Shortly a weak knock sounded at Jeno's door. Oiro, the youngest crew member, stuck his head in and said, "We're sorry, Jeno."

Jeno said gently, "Go to bed, Oiro. Hey—shut the door."

Jeno's hands found his genitals; he wanted desperately to experience their pleasure potential now that he knew he had them, but that, it seemed, would have to wait. He leaned over and lifted his intercom box from its place beside the bed.

"Where is Eroi tonight?" he asked the night-shift communications officer.

"I think she's sleeping in the nurse's chamber."

"Connect me."

A faint hiss indicated that someone in the nursery had answered the call light.

"Eroi?"

"What do you want, Jeno?"

157

"I—just to thank you for your help. You were right. From what we told it, the computer had our trajectory as a straight line, ignoring the sun's—"

"I know. I watched the display in the recording room."

Apparently she was willing to talk; at least she had not broken the connection.

"Are you feeling better?" Jeno asked.

"I don't know."

"You sound fine," Jeno remarked innocently—then realized he should have avoided reminding her of vocal changes to come. "Eroi, I need you. I don't think I can handle everything alone."

"You did well today. And I helped, didn't I?"

"Minimally."

"See?" she said angrily. "In your mind I'm already a slave. I owed you *this*; I let you down because of *that*!"

"You let yourself down, Eroi. Whatever happened to staying alive? Remember—'As long as there's any chance at all, we can't just give up and die?' You said that to me before I even suggested we try what we're doing. If we fail because you're off pouting somewhere—"

"Women and children pout," she interrupted him accusingly; "men are troubled and they go off to contemplate."

Jeno laughed, not happily. "You haven't changed," he said. Static was his only reply. "Tell me, Eroi, is your mind less efficient? Tell me honestly. Introspect."

No reply.

"Is learning less important to you? Does the future hold less promise?"

She answered this time. "Oh yes, Jeno, much less promise."

In spite of his serious attempt to see life from her new perspective, he was hurt by her implicit attitude toward

158

him and their past friendship. "Have you lost your memory?" he asked her as dispassionately as he could. "Don't you remember who I am—what I think—what I think of you? Isn't it obvious what I would do for you as your husband—what freedoms you would not even have to ask me for?" He did not add: Don't you see that there can be no other wife for me, ever?

She seemed to sense his dismay; she answered: "I remember us as equals, Jeno, as men-to-be for whom the worlds, the ship, the knowledge in the computers held no secrets and presented no obstacles. I remember our daring raids during the night to find out things that were forbidden, and our elaborate experiments to—"

"With all our experiments," he interrupted, "there was one we never thought would be available to us. It is now. If you will only come to terms with the way things are."

His meaning escaped her for a few seconds. "No!" she finally said, and abruptly shut off her intercom.

He extinguished his cabin lights. He lay there continuing to explore his body, imagining his hands were her hands, until his flesh began to send insistent messages to his brain and a lightning bolt of incredible pleasure stuck his entire body. He shouted in astonishment at his first experience of a pleasure he had only heard about, and the intercom box crashed to the floor.

Dell's voice outside his door startled him.

"Jeno! What's wrong?"

You wouldn't believe me if I told you, Jeno thought, laughing to himself. He called back, "Nothing, Dell, thank you. It was just—just a dream."

Chapter 13

Three Friends

The mid-course burn was accomplished fairly smoothly because Jeno relied almost as heavily on the Guardian computer system as he had done on the occasion of their first acceleration—the burn that yanked them free of planet five and sent them spiraling in toward three. He had hoped the children could learn in time to pilot the ship without the limited Guardian; they had not. He had hoped his crew would by then be adept at handling quick emergency maneuvers; they were not. He had hoped to be ready to command evasive action if Himi's ship should find them; he was not. He continued to have nightmares remembering the message Reno had sent offering to help them, while in the background of the picture an unconscious Himi was not taking part in a decision to "seek out and destroy."

"Don't worry," Pata had once tried to reassure Jeno; "they are *months* behind us!"

But were they? Were they even still in pursuit? It had always seemed ridiculous to Jeno that they would bother with such an expensive extermination; perhaps they had thought better of it and continued on their way. That was logical, but Jeno did not believe it—not if Fera was in charge now. Jeno's father had spoken often of the "evil" Fera, usually when expressing relief that there was not such a power-hungry villain aboard *his* happy ship—a ship now piloted by a handful of ignorant children. Jeno continued to push them through long hours of daily study and tedious drills. A few of them seemed to be coming along. . . .

"All present," Pata-Hald reported, "except Eroi, of course."

"She's—cleaning the galley," Dell reported sheepishly.

Pata quipped, "You've got to admit it needed it!"

"I'm sleepy," said little Oiro; "and I need some water."

Jeno asked, "Do you want a few minutes before we start? I know you're all tired and hungry and thirsty. But this has to be done."

"No," said Zena, "I want to get it over with. How long will it take?"

Jeno shook his head; "I don't know." He added with a shrug, "Take a vote."

"Let's vote on whether to do the drill at all or not," suggested Zeno.

Jeno smiled. "That's not in question."

"It is now," Pata announced self-righteously. "We don't believe in all this work, Jeno; we think the Guardian can do what needs to be done. And when we leave here, we still have to work in the gardens. We're tired."

"And frustrated," Jeno added for his younger relative.

"And entitled to our rights," said Pata.

"And mistaken, if you think this ship is still running as a strict democracy. It isn't."

"No," said Pata, accusingly, "you're our dictator."

Jeno laid his arm around Pata's shoulders; Pata seemed to welcome the gesture. "That's true," Jeno said, smiling. "It has to be that way—for a while, at least. You see why, don't you?"

There was no specific answer; silence indicated assent.

"I could have had ten drinks of water by now," Oiro said.

"Run get one, quick," said Jeno. "Today," he addressed his gathering, "we're all working on the communications console. We can't afford the luxury of specialization, not with only 17 of us running everything. First I have some—warnings and advice. I don't want anybody passing out at the sight of our first alien face on these monitors. We *will* contact them. We *will* learn to talk with them. They might be grotesque and sinister looking, they might be non-descript blobs of fur—who knows? They might already know we're coming; maybe they don't. We're in for some surprises, but I want you all to take them as *expected* surprises. They might even be hostile and try to shoot us down. If they do, no Guardian system will come to our rescue except for only basic maneuvers. *We have to stay awake!* Here's a container of stimulants that ought to help us if we get too excited or frightened, but I have no idea what the dosage ought to be for children. I've split these in half, notice; and every time we have a drill from now on, I want one of you, only one, to take the drug so we can learn our tolerances. Pata—you first."

Pata seemed to feel honored to be first, and eager to do something adults did. He popped half a tablet in his mouth with flourish.

Oiro returned at a gallop—he was still small enough to

be able to make better time on all fours.

"What's this?" Jeno asked his group, pointing to a large red button.

Several answered in unison, "The distress beacon. *Never touch the distress beacon!*"

"And this . . . and this . . . and this . . ." he continued his quiz, filling in the blanks when he got no responses at all. "Dell, aim the directional antenna at planet three; then, Taza, warm up the receiver."

"What channel?"

"You tell me."

"All channels? Okay, how do you set up a full-spectrum scan?"

Jeno challenged, "Pata, can you answer Taza's question?"

Pata tried, but his instruction fell short; he knew only part of it. Jeno conscientiously refrained from expressing disappointment and made the adjustments himself.

Instantly a quasi-picture appeared on one of the nine displays. It was shadowy with no color and no definition, but it looked like it might have been a man sitting at a desk. The picture changed abruptly into what might have been a landscape. Then . . .

"Why is the picture fading away?" Pata asked.

Eroi's voice came from the intercom: "Because you have not stabilized the outer shell of the ship. If you don't do that, we'll be sending our answering signal everywhere, and Himi's people will locate us—if they haven't already."

Dell got a nod from Jeno and rushed to the propulsion console to adjust the outer shell's attitude.

"Where are you?" Jeno demanded of Eroi.

"In the recording room."

"Come to the command center."

"No."

163

"I'm giving you only two choices, Eroi: either come to the center and assume your responsibilities or be confined, imprisoned, with no freedom of movement and only sustenance nourishment—indefinitely."

"I'm doing the duties expected of me," she replied lightly.

"Not the ones *I* expect of you." Jeno was gambling. It seemed possible to him that she might prefer solitary confinement to masculine duty. This also would mean that she would have to break her self-imposed solitary and let herself be seen.

He did not know her choice until she emerged from the stairway in the floor within a few paces of the communications console. There were a number of gasps. She looked angry and humiliated and yet showed no signs of dizziness; she was an exceptionally beautiful woman; and she was dressed as a man.

"I despise you for this, Jeno," she snarled; her voice had changed too: despite the emotional intensity, it was softer and higher. Thoroughly feminine.

"Sit down," he ordered her. "Pata, give her your chair."

"I will not!" Pata protested. "Jeno, that's insane!"

Jeno lifted the youngster bodily from his chair and motioned with his head for Eroi to be seated. Jeno did not say it, but his actions conveyed to all: now watch someone who knows what she's doing.

"We're stable now," Dell shouted.

Eroi studied the controls, adjusted various settings, and returned the missing foggy picture to the monitor. "I think that's just a stray terrestrial picture," she said. "Nothing deliberately directed at us. Anything else? May I go now?"

"Sharpen the image," Jeno commanded.

She complied. Now they knew what the aliens looked like: slender, burdened with excessive clothing ("Perhaps

164

it's winter," Taza observed) and very simple biologically. It was difficult to see how they managed with so few bones, joints, and fingers. Yet they moved spastically, as if the picture were speeded up ("There's something about the speed of light and relative velocities that might do that," Jeno observed). The picture faded away again.

Eroi adjusted more dials and consulted the computer. "The world has turned so that the source of the signal is no longer in our line of sight. I think. Now may I go?"

"You will receive a new duty roster tonight," Jeno said to her, "which will require your presence here a certain number of hours every day. Yes, you may go back to the nursery, or the galley, or wherever you feel at home."

Eroi was at the console a few weeks later, studying a row of empty monitors, when suddenly the frames thereon flopped a number of times until all of them held a remarkable image, one that needed no sharpening at all. "Jeno!" she called, excited in spite of herself. "Look!"

There was one of the creatures, even more encrusted with clothing than others had been, with a brown hat on his head. He was speaking—they could hear it—in a twittering clicking tongue.

"It's highly directional, I'm sure," Eroi said, "and I think it's sent right to us. I think they know we're here!"

As if answering her supposition, the picture split in half; on one side there was the hatted alien and on the other was a star field with a single moving faint star. The image of the star became larger as a zooming action took place; soon it could be seen that the star was a tiny crescent dot.

"Can we check out the star field behind that crescent?" Jeno asked. "Find out where in space, relative to planet three, it is?"

Eroi said: "You think that's a picture of us, don't you?"

165

"It might be. They might be specifically wanting to tell us they see us."

"I'm afraid that's too complicated for me," Eroi said. "It would take me hours to figure out how to do it."

The creature in the picture stopped chattering and threw out his arms in an obvious gesture of welcome—or so it seemed. Then the transmission was terminated.

"We've got to answer them—now!" said Eroi.

Jeno nodded. "Soon, anyway," he half agreed. "Pata, I have a project for you, and two others you can choose to help you. I want as complete a profile on that planet—let's call it Three—as you can develop with the sensors we've got. There's an old profile in the data bank, but I don't trust it. We need to know it's size, shape, weight, atmospheric content, length of day, length of year, and all those kinds of things."

"Jeno," Eroi prodded. "Answer them!"

"I don't know *how* to answer them," Jeno said impatiently. "What do we say? How do we say it?"

"If we don't answer them soon, we may lose line of sight with their transmitter," Eroi explained.

"I realize that," Jeno retorted. "That's what made me think of getting a profile on the planet. We don't know how fast it revolves, so we don't know how much time we have for a fast reply. Besides, they might be able to receive and relay messages from all over their world, so line of sight might not matter all that much."

"If we don't do something quick, Jeno," Eroi pleaded, "they won't know we're responding to their signal." Eroi slammed her hand down on the console. A loud buzz went off that showed she had activated the distress beacon.

"Turn that off!" Jeno fairly screamed at her.

She did as she was told.

The children looked at one another in terror. Dizziness

began to overcome some of them. Eroi had betrayed their location to Himi's ship! Pata fumbled for the drug that might keep him going; he physically shoved Eroi out of her chair and took it over. "You had to put a woman in charge!" Pata screamed at Jeno.

Eroi got to her feet. She did not seem angry or particularly insulted. She had expected this reaction from Pata and the others, probably Jeno too. "I assumed," she said to Jeno, "that by now Himi already knows where we are. He would be stupid if he did not. The distress beacon is omni-directional and automatically scans all frequencies. The people on Three now know we heard them. Shall I consider myself under arrest?"

"What do you suggest we do next?" Jeno asked.

"Send them a picture. Let them know we *saw* them as well and that we are ready to correspond."

"A picture of what?"

"It doesn't matter. Anything."

Jeno tapped Pata's shoulder. "Give Eroi her seat back," he ordered.

Pata stood, incredulity on his face, and made a dignified protest exit down the stairs.

"Set the main camera," Jeno ordered Eroi. "We will show them what we look like. Come close, children—men."

Oiro and Mara crawled speedily toward the camera as the internal monitor showed that their family portrait was being sent to Three, to the man with the hat.

Jeno's door was banged open in the middle of the night; he had been sleeping soundly. Dell said, "Wake up, Jeno; Mara's gone!"

"Gone where?"

"To—we think he's gone to the outersphere."

167

Jeno leapt from the bed, his head spinning. "Why? What makes you think that? Where have you looked?"

"He's been talking about going there," Dell admitted shamefully. "We didn't tell you because ... well, because—"

"Tell me," Jeno insisted as he and the little one rushed out into the corridor leading to the command center stairs.

"He kept saying you and Eroi had murdered everybody or maybe just locked them all in the outersphere so you could take over the ship. We've all told him he's crazy. But he—"

"Did you check to see whether a suit's missing?"

"There is one missing."

Jeno stopped short. "Dell, go to the center; tell whoever's on the intercom to keep trying to get him to answer. Maybe he's got his suit radio on. Tell him that if he enters the outersphere he can never come back. Yes, I know that's a frightening idea, but it's the truth. If he comes back he could kill us all. I'm going to try to stop him. Oh, and wake up Eroi. Get her to find out if there's a way for us here to seal the outersphere airlocks. Maybe we can keep him from entering." Or perhaps from leaving it again, if he's already entered, Jeno thought.

A suit was indeed missing from the cabinet. Jeno grabbed one for himself—then remembered something in his father's explanation to Himi, something about dormant cells even in the vacuum of the innersphere. Forlornly he let the suit fall to the floor. There was nothing he could do.

He contacted Eroi, who was by this time in the command center. "There is an emergency switch in the innersphere that allows someone out there to enter the nucleusphere lock," he told her; "override it. Lock that door permanently. Are there others there with you?"

"Yes, almost everybody."

"Leave them there. Have them continue to try and reach Mara on the intercom. You meet me in the upper corridor at the base of the stairs."

She looked pale and worried when he saw her. "We contacted Mara," she told Jeno. "He has been to the outersphere. They are all dead. His—his parents are dead. And this gray stuff is all around. He's terribly frightened. He wants to come home."

Jeno shook his head. "Did you seal the nucleusphere lock?"

"Yes."

"You understand the problem?"

"Yes."

"But there's one more thing. He will wait for us to let him in—until he dies. Probably of starvation before the parasite kills him. Then his body will float free in the innersphere. If we allow that to happen, we'll be in constant danger that his body will drift into some moving part. We have to get him to go back into the outersphere, of his own accord. Can you help me do it?"

"Yes."

"You found a way to activate the outersphere systems?"

"Yes." She handed him a small portable intercom. He switched it on.

"Oh, please let me in, Jeno," said a small voice. "I'm sorry. I won't do it again. I'm so scared! It's dark here, and there's all this machinery. And I'm feeling sick, I—"

Jeno switched it off. "Can the other children hear this?" She nodded.

"Go move them to where they can't. But you listen." She seemed decidedly unsteady on her feet, but she looked Jeno straight in the eye and said, "All right."

Jeno felt his pocket. He had no stimulants.

When Eroi had returned up the stairs, Jeno opened the intercom two-way. "Mara, this is Jeno."

"Oh, Jeno! I thought you didn't hear me! I'm caught in the innersphere; please let me in!"

"What you did was very wrong, you realize that, don't you?"

"I won't do it again!"

"There's something I want you to do for me. Will you?"

"What is it?"

"First, I know it's pretty dark in there; but you can make it brighter. Are you near the nucleusphere airlock?"

"Yes, my hand is on the wheel of it."

"See that square metal box—right on the door. It has two switches on it. Turn one of them on. Did the light get brighter?"

"Yes."

"Now I want you to float back over to the outersphere—watch out for the cables and the flywheels—and open the door of the lock you used before."

"No! Jeno I can't!"

"I don't want you to go any farther than the lock. In the lock there's a control panel that regulates the airflow. Call me when you're over there and in front of that panel. We need to have some adjustments made, and you're the only one who can do it."

There was a long wait, perhaps while Mara mustered the courage and then made another dangerous leap across the gulf separating the two mammoth spheres which turned on axes perpendicular to one another. It would be a harrowing trip for even an explorer to make. "I'm here, Jeno," the little voice said at last.

Jeno switched off his intercom. "*Now,* Eroi!" he shouted, as he bounded up the stairs. But his legs buckled and he fell, semi-conscious, at the top step. He next felt the cold pressure of an alcohol towel against his neck. Dell was administering it. He looked to Eroi's station and saw that she was being cared for by the twins.

"Mara's dead, isn't he?" Dell asked.

"Are all the kids here?" Jeno asked him.

"Yes. They want to know."

"He's not dead," Pata said. He was standing by the intercom controls; he flipped a switch and Mara's voice entered the command center: "I'm locked in! Oh, please let me out! Jeno! Jeno!"

"Shut that off," Jeno commanded Pata.

"Yes, master." Pata saw that he had chosen a wrong time to needle. "We want all of the truth, Jeno. We may be children, but we're the best men you've got. We want to see Hald's tape."

Jeno nodded.

"It's almost time for our regular contact with Three," Eroi said, wakening.

"I think it's time we showed *them* the tape too," Jeno said. "Perhaps they will recognize the gray stuff and will know what to do about it. Eroi, load up and begin to show the tape; when Three time comes, just cut in, wherever we are, so they can see it. Okay, I want each of you to take half a stimulant. What you're about to see is terrible. But, you'll see, it bears out what I have already explained to you. This is the whole truth."

That night, long after the shifts had changed and Jeno was at last in bed—wondering why so little progress was being made in understanding the aliens' speech—he heard a weak tap at his door.

"Come in?"

171

It was Oiro. He stepped timidly to Jeno's bedside and said, "I can't sleep. I'm scared."

Jeno raised the corner of his sheet. "Hop in," he invited.

Knowledge was being exchanged even though a direct method of communication had not been devised.

"Their symbol for the number 4 looks sort of like ours," Dell observed. "But what are all those funny check marks and tiny things that surely are not numbers? That equation looks like it has numbers and pictures all mixed together."

Eroi pointed to the screen. "That's the person who makes the best sense. He's systematic. See—he's showing a picture of a hand and, I guess saying their word for it. Can any of you make out the word? Even when we put the picture back on their speed, it just sounds like twittering to me."

"Twittering to me too," said Jeno.

So they called him Twitter. They had seen Hat again too—the man who had first contacted them. Twitter's assistant, who had longer hair than the other two men, came to be known as Hair. Hat, Twitter, and Hair, their friends on Three.

As they drew closer to the planet, more and more different men spoke to them, but their friends continued to capture attention best. A mystique had instantly surrounded Hat, Twitter and Hair; these were the three smart enough to contact them in the first place; these were the three who were there almost every day and who seemed most intent upon learning to speak to their approaching visitors. These, surely, would be the three who could save them. Besides, Twitter and Hair smiled and once even laughed: they looked like fun.

But the pictures they sent flashed by so fast! How could anyone be expected to take in so much at a time? Jeno had deduced: "I think they're compressing time, assuming we have a computer that can spread it out again. Eroi, program gaps between each of their frames." She had objected: "But that will break up the continuity of their speech. We'll *never* understand them that way." But Jeno had won, and the adjustment had been made. The pictures took on new importance instantly. Given time to study them, the crew members gasped at wonders and beauties of which they had never dreamed:

Lofty cities, mountains even taller, forests everywhere apparently, airplanes that must have been capable of carrying half a thousand passengers, highway systems that looked from above like tangles of twine, people in crowds, people in groups, people in pairs, and people alone—and the diversity of it all! No two garments alike! No two buildings alike! No two cities alike! It was the architecture that overwhelmed them the most: it looked as if Three had to be a planetary crossroads where myriad alien races coexisted. Yet except for minor variations in skin color, all the inhabitants seemed to be of the same species.

Jeno shook his head in amazement. "They'll want us to show them pictures of our planet too," he murmured. "I'm embarrassed to do it."

But the experience was not as humiliating as Jeno feared it might be. Watching their own telecasts, they regained a pride in their planetary heritage. Exchanging points of view with the aliens, they realized that quite a story of their own history could be gleaned from the pictures. An aerial photograph taken over a large brown lake showed a port city that stretched back to the horizon. As the camera came in closer, over great flat barges, the rows of buildings at the coast became distinct. They were hill-like fortresses clearly built and repeatedly reinforced over eons, changed as new methods and materials were voted into use: the wide-spread bottom stories were of rock and clay; the few stories above them were manufactured blocks and mortar; above that were stories made of wood and concrete with elaborate carvings; next came a few stories made of combinations of the previous methods; and finally, crowning the tops of many of them, there was glittering steel, gold, aluminum and other metals—inlaid with jewel-like quartz windows. The buildings and streets were in fine repair. People on foot and in uniform box-like automobiles moved about purposefully.

Jeno selected a tape of the construction and launching of Hald's and Himi's ships. It compared rather favorably, he thought, with pictures Three had sent showing pen-shaped rockets and tiny spacecraft that looked like airplanes—all hovering around a huge structure under construction in space. Were they, too, preparing to launch an exploratory ship to look for habitable planets? If they were, Jeno could not fathom why—because there was an incredible amount of growing space left on the breathtakingly beautiful planet. A planet of electricity, Jeno called it, because there were lights and moving machines everywhere!

"There's no point in showing them any more of our cities," Jeno mentioned, one day while they were stumped for a next presentation; "they all look alike."

"They've shown us their living quarters," Pata said, "why not show them our planet's?"

Jeno laughed. "I'm not sure they'll even recognize that's what we're showing them. Beds, kitchens, and hallways to the work-trains. That's all we have."

"Let's show them," Pata joked, "a tape of the puppet sex show."

Jeno laughed, then thought: "Let's do. Perhaps they will return the favor. I'm curious, aren't you?"

Following Three's reply to the puppet show, Eroi livened up considerably. She began to appear in the command center even when not summoned, and her behavior toward Jeno took on some of the familiarity they had established in childhood. In studying Three's reply, Eroi had learned that many of those assumed to be men were in fact women—responsible women—who lived and worked as Three's men did. The children of Three were born without shells, their sex visible from birth; and their education was begun at once.

"Hair," Eroi announced triumphantly, "is a woman!"

A strange broadcast was picked up from random signals reaching the ship (the nearer they got, the more of these local Three stations they could occasionally pick up). It showed women wearing large exquisitely decorated dresses and men riding on swift and streamlined beasts of burden. The only buildings shown were simple wooden ones. And there were odd interruptions: short scenes showing highly sophisticated automobiles and towering modern buildings. The last shot in the sequence was always of a man standing beside one of the cars which was positioned on a moving colorful floor. These pictures of machines had no apparent connection with the action of men and beasts.

"It's a story!" little Eroi squealed, "like nurses tell!"

"Do you suppose they can travel back in time?" Pata whispered.

"This must be a story about their invention of electric cars," Jeno deduced.

For Jeno, Eroi, and their fourteen diminutive crew

175

members, lessons became a joy, work an exciting pastime, and sleep a regrettable necessity. The computer had set for them a time each day that allowed for the turning of the planet, sleep schedules aboard the ship, and the probability that most crew members could be present at most conversations. That short time each day was a celebration of wonder, a gleeful test of logical powers, and a tearful realization of hope. They had lost all trace of doubt that the people of Three might know how to save them.

"I've taken so many stimulants," Jeno checkled, "that I feel like my limbs will just crack and fall off."

Eroi laughed gaily. "Me too, but there's nothing to worry about. I've checked your orbit over and over. It should put us in a synchronous position right over Hat, Twitter and Hair. And when they invite us to land, we just push a button!"

Jeno and Eroi had studied the orbit and landing sequences Hald had programmed for their last planetary stop—the deadly one—and trusted the Guardian to adapt it to Three's slightly different gravity and rotational speed. The spheres were not arrested—as they had been for their powerful mid-course burn—but were spinning even faster than usual, in anticipation of maneuvers within the atmosphere. On the masterscope, a large completely spherical moon was slipping at a visible rate behind the planet.

Suddenly the picture of Three slid up diagonally, to be replaced by a field of stars when the picture was again stabilized. The Guardian had instructed the outer shell and the attitude rockets to position the ship for orbital insertion.

When the explosion came, Pata screamed. It was not a

scream of terror but an attempt to share a stupendous hair-raising thrill. The twins returned the screech. Before the maneuver had been completed, everyone had joined in the shout-and-laughter festivity.

In a flash, an enormous piece of space hardware appeared on the masterscope. "What's that?" Eroi shouted. No one knew, and before an answer could even be guessed at it was gone. "Did we hit it?" she asked.

"I don't know," said Jeno. "Are the deflectors working?"

"They are now," she said. "Came on automatically, I guess." She added with a shrug: "Good old Guardian."

The picture on the masterscope at last showed slowly drifting cloud formations and a great stationary land mass below.

"We're in orbit," said Jeno with an unstoppable grin.

Chapter 14

The Landing

"Jeno," Dell called out; he had to shout over the whir of the rapidly spinning nucleusphere, "I'm getting little bumps all over my hands."

"Me too," said Pata.

"They itch!" said the twins in unison.

Jeno laughed. "You're lucky it's just your hands. Look at my arms! It's a rash caused by too much excitement, I think. Don't scratch; that'll probably make it worse. Try to think of ordinary things. Here, study your arithmetic—" He punched up a video display that was visible to most and instructed it to run a series of problems for mental exercise.

"I have to urinate," Oiro said, a little frantically.

Jeno laughed. "Not *that* ordinary, men. Sorry, Oiro, nobody leaves his chair until we have some idea whether we're to land at once, orbit for a while longer, or orbit indefinitely."

"Look—that's a ship of some kind, isn't it?" Eroi was pointing at a bright dot moving just above the dark side of the terminator below.

"Coming to meet us?" Jeno wondered. He ordered Eroi: "Open all typical Three frequencies. Maybe Hat or Twitter or Hair is on that ship; maybe they will try to speak to us and tell us what to do."

"How will we understand them?" Eroi asked.

"They know we can't exchange words with them, so perhaps they will send us a picture or a diagram we can interpret."

"I'm getting something."

"Put it on the masterscope."

The picture was of half a sphere, with stars moving behind it. "He's sending back a picture of us," Jeno said.

"Why are we cut in half?" Sanz asked, then realized: "Oh, the sunlight—"

Jeno ordered: "Eroi, split the screen so we can watch them as they watch us." He added, "Instruct our cameras to—"

"Follow their ship? I wish I could. I don't know how to do that with an object at close range. It has something to do with a heat-sensing targeter, but—"

"Can you do it manually?"

"I think so, most of the time."

Jeno—checking figures on a sheaf of copious notes—typed coordinates into the navigation computer. "Just a hunch," he said to Eroi. "If they ask us to land, I've got a feeling we'll be directed to where our friends have their transmitter. I've asked it to land us there."

"I'm getting a second picture from their scout ship," Eroi said. She punched it up on the masterscope; it took up half of the space previously occupied by the first alien signal. It was a closer view of themselves.

"Scout ship is right," Jeno agreed. "It's looking us over, making sure we can land safely, perhaps seeing that we carry no external armaments—none that show, anyway. Isn't there sound with the pictures?"

"Just the usual twittering."

"It's a beautiful little space ship, isn't it?" Zeno muttered to his twin when the image of it was close and large on the screen.

"Of course," said Zena, "everything here is beautiful!"

"Look! It's taking a picture of our camera—a picture of us taking a picture of them taking a picture of us!" shouted Zeno.

"This is quite a situation!" said Pata, laughing.

Suddenly all three of the masterscope's pictures were obliterated and replaced by one multi-band transmission. In the three identical pictures, Hat was standing at the front of an enormous group of people. He bent one knee and touched it to the floor. Those behind him did the same. He threw out his arms in what seemed a gesture of welcome. The others followed his lead. As suddenly as it had appeared, the picture vanished. The scout ship was no longer in sight.

"Hold onto your seats!" Jeno shouted as he activated the landing sequence.

They felt the nucleusphere strain to pick up rotational speed just before the gradual burn began to tug at them. On the blast, Eroi's dials confirmed that Hat's message had indeed originated at the exact spot expected—just to the north of their orbital position.

They were landing!

While the masterscope showed a rapidly ballooning planet, the children chanted off the major numerals on the projected altimeter: "...12,000...11,000...10,000...9,000...." They were growing short of breath and their

180

mouths worked none too well under the combined forces of acceleration and centrifuge. If anyone was frightened for his life, no one indicated it—not even little Oiro, who chanted more loudly than most.

Jeno kept his worries to himself. They were drifting inexplicably westward. He hoped the Guardian knew what it was doing. They broke through wonderful and harmless towers of clouds; below them was a vast expanse of ocean with no land in sight. Jeno popped two full tablets of stimulant into his mouth and labored hard to swallow them.

Eroi switched the masterscope view to show another direction. "What are those?" she asked.

Three bright dots seemed to be approaching them at tremendous speed. The next blurred image showed that they were slender rods with fiery tails; then after dissolving into three long smudges, they were gone.

"They're celebrating our arrival!" Eroi speculated.

"I—probably so," Jeno said; he was eyeing the control light that indicated the deflector screen had briefly been energized.

The acceleration force ended unexpectedly. An ensuing sense of vertigo was amplified when the nucleusphere shuddered, straining against new forces tugging at it. The masterscope showed only streaks of light and shade.

"The outer shell is beginning to spin," Jeno shouted in explanation to the anxious faces turned toward him. "We're deep into the air now and we're maneuvering with vanes extending outward from the shell. The spheres must keep their established orientations, but the shell can turn any direction necessary. We seem to be making a turn that will take us back to the east. I hope."

The shuddering died down and again there was a burst

of acceleration. On the masterscope, a coastline appeared in the distance, became a smear, and overtook the deep blue of the ocean.

"Hey—it's getting dark ahead!" Sanz pointed out; but before he finished saying it, it *was* dark. "Look at all the li-iiiiiii!"

If they had not been securely strapped in, many might have been hauled from their chairs by the powerful sideways pull. The shell had spun again and they were heading straight up into the air. When the spin had stopped and the ship was oriented with its rockets pointing down, the masterscope showed the aft scene: an illuminated round radio dish nestled among dark mountains.

"The Guardian took us literally!" Jeno said, panicked; "it's going to land *on* the transmitter!"

Eroi called Jeno's attention to the dancing wave forms on one of her displays. "They're trying to talk to us, but it's just words!"

"Hang on tight," Jeno yelled. He quickly overrode the Guardian's program and reignited the thrusters full blast. The picture on the masterscope vanished in a spreading white glow from the rockets.

The controls were in Jeno's hands; he was piloting the ship manually, for all practical purposes, and the responsibility was too terrifying. His consciousness was flickering.

Eroi saw that the ship was again streaking westward. She saw Jeno's eyes close and his head bob tellingly. Before she herself fainted, she was able to switch off Jeno's Guardian override.

"What's wrong? What's happening? What's the situation?" The children were alarmed not by the action of the ship but by the terror they saw evidence of in their leaders.

182

Stimulants or no, they began to wink out and hang limp in their chairs.

When Jeno awoke, others were groaning to awareness around him.

The nucleusphere—the whine of it descending in pitch—was running down. Control modules and acceleration chairs had made full 90 degree shifts, and the catwalk—their new floor—was fully extended. The masterscope, now forming a domed ceiling, showed the quiet scene outside: a smouldering mountainside in the first light of dawn.

They had landed.

Part 4

LOOKING BEYOND

Chapter 15

Biological Bomb

Twice within a two-week period, spring rains fell in sheets over the mountains to the north of the aliens' landing site. Accumulating water drained off the peaks and sloshed across the desert floor—making rapids along normally dry river beds, cutting lightning-shaped trenches where the desert floor was softest, flushing through mountain passes like the run-off from a broken dam. At the site, Alienites and hordes of other curious onlookers moved their tents and prefabs to higher ground, encroaching even further on the NASA camp nestled in the protection of Twin Peaks.

Radioactive particles were plowed under, dispersed, washed southward, rendered less harmful; and the showers that spat over the site in large globules effectively cleansed the shell of the quiet, towering sphere. A round pool of water filled the atom-baked crater beneath the ship. Yellow poppies and magenta verbena—their seeds shocked into life by the deluge, mutated into hasty and exaggerated growth by the radiation—were already budding along the rim of the shallow crater lake.

A man in boots and dark dungarees, wearing a backpack, trudged through the coagulating mud of the Alienites camp. He was a stranger to those he passed, but he was friendly. He would say, "Evening, nice night, isn't it?" or "Looks like we've had the last of the rain," to those he passed. To the security guard at the periphery of the NASA camp, he said, "I'm with air traffic control, Tuscon, and I have urgent business with General McCook. I'll wait here while you check to see if he'll talk to me now. Please do not use your intercom; my presence here must not be generally known." He flashed convincing credentials, waited until the guard had his back turned at the door to the General's prefab, then scurried to the protection of shadows within the camp. He used a pen-light to illuminate an aerial photo of the NASA installation, picked out a nearby prefab, ran to it, and knocked politely on the door.

"Come in," said a voice the man was relieved to recognize as William Reid's.

His face-to-face greeting was neither hostile nor enthusiastic. Reid asked him: "How did you get past the guards?"

"Subterfuge."

"Gari, have you met Hal Gordon?" Reid asked his companion. "Unscrupulous but reasonably good writer for the New York Times. He did that hatchet job on Starprobe in support of your father's Blot."

The reporter smiled and nodded; "Dr. Copalin," he said simply. Gordon was suddenly worried. This was not the relatively passive William Reid he remembered; his task might not prove as simple as he had hoped.

"Join us for coffee, Hal," Reid said unexpectedly. "I'll

tell you what you want to know." He added: "But we'll have to be fast—get it over with before they come to cart you away."

Struggling with grunts and groans as he peeled off his boots, Gordon said, "There's been just too little information—"

"I know," said Reid; "I agree with you."

"They're saying ... well, Dr. Fauchelet in Paris thinks you're conspiring with the aliens. Corothers in D.C. claims he's deciphered their language, and the aliens are warning us they can destroy the earth. And Hillary—"

"Thinks the military is preparing to blast them to kingdom come. Corothers is probably right; Hillary's not far wrong. Cream and sugar?"

"You're kidding!" He switched on his recorder quickly. "Black." Gordon revved up his interviewer's mentality and began: "When did you first—?"

Reid interrupted him. "Just listen. I'll tell you everything I can. And here, take this with you." He scooped up a videotape from his workbench and tossed it to Gordon. "NASA and other governmental agencies are maintaining secrecy for a good reason, generally: we must communicate with the aliens in fragments; clarity is hard to come by. And there's no sense inviting a nervous public to speculate on ambiguous meanings, until we know more. But since so much speculation is going on already, I don't mind telling you some things.

"The aliens are metabolically slower than we are, and, apparently, they live considerably longer lives. Their home planet is larger and more massive than earth, but otherwise rather similar. They could breathe our air, eat our food, and from the pictorial analyses of body fluids they have transmitted, their natural immunities would counteract most of our diseases. They do have a different body chemistry, however, and their reduced hemoglobin

186

and almost exoskeleton-like skins make them less sensitive to radiation—much less. I'm convinced they had no idea what danger their propulsion system posed to us."

"Their mission here?" Gordon asked.

"I don't think they have one," Reid said with a shrug. "I get the impression they were not even supposed to have contacted us—much less landed. I don't know... curiosity, perhaps, brought them to us."

"What about—?"

"I can tell you much more if you don't interrupt, Hal. We *have* learned to communicate with them—in a terribly complicated way. The difference in our... metabolism isn't the right word exactly, speed of mental response is more to the point, causes us to have to use computers and other electronic interfaces. We have to slow our own speech for them, and accelerate theirs for us—while keeping the vocal tones roughly unaltered in pitch. It can take us an hour just to exchange a few words. Most of our data concerning them comes from schematics and photographs they send.

"We have a fairly extensive vocabulary of nouns—parts of the body, names of things we can picture. Ostensive definitions. And we're beginning to collect their words for qualitative concepts—like pleasure, pain, hunger, good, bad, and so on. A misunderstanding of even the simplest sort can make us lose a whole day of work. Their day, incidentally, is close enough to ours that they have been able to sleep when we sleep and work when we work. They seem as anxious as we are to learn to communicate.

"Dr. Corothers must have picked up our 'conversation' with the aliens a couple of days ago—in which we learned, with reasonable certainty, their words for *danger*, *trouble*, and *all-destructive*. We think they also used a word that could be interpreted as *warning*. There are a great many ways to read their possible meanings. From other things we think we understand, I tend to believe that they are warning us to be wary of their sister ship. They don't know where it is either, by the way; and they seem to be afraid of being found by it.

"I don't know yet why—or even if I understand them correctly about this—but they do not seem anxious to leave their ship. Asked if they needed us to open their hatches from the outside, they replied with a repeated and emphatic string of no's."

The knock at the door was timid. "Dr. Reid?" a voice called out; "we have an intruder. May I—?"

"He's here," Reid answered; "come in."

Gordon had stashed the recorder and Reid's videotape in his backpack before the two guards opened the door.

"His name is Hal Gordon," Reid told the guards, "and he's a personal friend of mine. He was afraid you wouldn't let him in if he told you only that. Go easy on him."

"You know the restrictions, Dr. Reid," the guard admonished.

Gordon was inwardly relieved; although Reid had been reprimanded, it had been done by an underling reminding some royal personage of a point of protocol.

"Well," said Gordon, rising to leave, "I'm very glad we got to visit for a few minutes, Bill. Thanks for not turning me in right away."

Gari handed the reporter a scrap of paper. On it was written: "Their captain's name, pronounced as it sounds to us, is *Jeno*. His next-in-command is a woman, *Eroi*."

Gordon's face radiated delight, amusement, and the excitement of someone who has just won a million-dollar state lottery. "Thanks," he tried to say expressionlessly. Gari had given him a terrific human-interest lead for his story.

"What's the latest on Bud?" William asked, stopping Gordon at the door.

"They released him this morning from Baylor Hospital. I don't think the prognosis is terrific, but the doctors are being evasive."

Reid nodded somberly.

"I'm afraid you'll have to come with us, Mr. Gordon," said the guard who had heretofore remained silent. His partner looked at him questioningly.

"This guy's not a personal friend of Reid's," the guard explained, not caring that he was being overheard by Gordon. "Reid's friends call him William, not Bill. And that 'doctors are being evasive' is how a reporter would look at it." They were marching Gordon toward the military administration hut. "Reid might be the golden boy around here," the guard continued, "but he's not in charge of the operation. And some people are getting suspicious of him, I hear. He lied to *us*, after all."

"I'm making a sandwich, Gari. Want one?"

"Yes, but you're going to find the bread missing."

"You don't suppose Ganymede—?"

"She might eat the food, but not the wrappers. Last time I checked there were plenty of those instant-dinner things. Peel me one, would you?"

"I don't see them." William had been standing on a plastic equipment crate peering into high kitchen cabinets. He jumped down and barked angrily, "Goddamn it, I'm going to hire 24-hour security for this place. We have too much to worry about without having to track down a food thief."

"We've *got* 24-hour security," Gari said, joining him. "Maybe the thief is one of them. It's probably someone from the Alienite camp, but I don't see how they're getting in and out. You're sure we're not walking and eating in our sleep?"

"This is not a joke," William said angrily.

"Go back to work; I'll find us something to eat."

"Ganymede?" Reid yelled. He seemed to expect her to come running with instant-dinner wrapper sticking incriminatingly out of her mouth.

"She's still tied outside," Gari said, stressing her own calm to dramatize William's lack of it. "Want me to bring her in?"

William nodded gratefully. "I'm sorry," he added.

The front door was open, Gari had been outside for more than a minute, and Ganymede still had not come bounding cheerfully into the hut. "William?" Gari called from out in the dark somewhere; "You'd better come out here."

The leash was still tied to the ring in the styrene siding of the hut, but Ganymede was not attached to the other end of it.

"Someone let her go," William said, quietly expressing horror and disbelief.

Word was circulated by intercom in the NASA camp and by telephone down to the Alienites. No one had seen Ganymede. Just after midnight, William was trying—with moderate success—to keep his mind on work (he was modifying a tone synthesizer in the hope of expediting translations of the alien tongue) when there was a soft knock at his door. It seemed apologetic in advance; and William instantly feared it was someone to tell him Ganymede's body had been found.

It was Bud Sullivan, most of his face burned and bandaged; he was wearing heavy winter outer-garments to protect his hypersensitive skin against the cool desert air. "Hi," he said.

Tears gushed out of William's tired eyes.

"Don't cry," Bud said. "It's so typical of you that it will make me laugh—and that hurts."

Gari came into the room and wrapped her arms around Bud's waist.

"Not too tight, love," he warned. "I'm molting."

William wiped his eyes with his palms. "Why are you here?" he asked Bud, frowning.

"Why not?" Bud responded jovially. "They can't do anything more for me at the hospital. And I can 'wait and see' here as well as there."

"How long do you have to live?" William asked; there was a cruel bitterness in his voice.

"Do you know something I don't?" Bud replied. "The doctors say I have a chance; they're trying some new drug from Sweden that's supposed to restore damaged cells. Am I going to die, William?"

William began to cry again. "You stupid bastard," he growled; "what did you think you were doing up there?"

"Shut up, William," Gari demanded.

Bud was listening as if trying to understand some arcane equation. "It was my life," he suggested.

"No," said William, "not entirely. Part of it was mine. Part of it was Gari's. They said you weren't even wearing your helmet!"

"I managed to get it on before I passed out."

"A lot of good that did. Your cabin didn't have a pressure leak. The damage had been done. The windows, for God's sake! You had your viewports unshielded!"

Bud listened to William's stifled sobbing a moment.

191

"William, I'm sorry," he said gently. "I'd better not stay."

William squeezed his forehead as if trying to ward off a headache. "You *have* to stay. There's room here, and we have a good infirmary with doctors who know everything there is to know about radiation sickness. Forgive me, please. You're the only person in my life I've ever wanted to hit."

"Good thing I'm wearing bandages. I'm going for a walk while you cool down. Maybe I can get a look at the big mother now that she's landed."

Gari nodded. "Walk around the base of the mountain toward the west. You can see it through the pass. Don't be gone long, and don't get too close."

"I won't."

Tall as the mountains surrounding it, lighted with beams situated on the peaks and in the arroyo, there stood the iron bubble that had caused 27 known deaths during its landing. Seeing it again, Bud was awestruck: it looked much larger on earth than it had in space. He marveled that the death toll had not been greater. You're right, Billy-Boy, Bud thought, I was a stupid bastard.

The thing was held out of the crater pool on curving sections that had folded down from the outer shell. It looked like a great seed perched on delicate flower petals. There was little wind to ripple the water, and a clear reflection showed Bud that the lethal rocket nozzle was not only retracted but was sealed over with a spherical section of metal.

The monster was silent. Bud heard only indistinct human voices (they were erecting some kind of housing down there), remote howls of coyotes, chirping insects, and the sizzle of breezes strumming charred twigs and new grasses. He lay back, his hands under his head, and looked at the stars. The Milky Way was an incandescent cloud, and the minor stars were so bright that it was difficult to pick out the constellations.

People out there. Endless varieties and species. All of them with ideas of their own. Histories of their own. Gods of their own. Bud thought of the times when mankind's concepts of the heavens had changed cataclysmically—a flat earth supported by elephants (standing on what? Bud wondered), the Greeks with their round earth and concentric spheres of planets and stars, sun-centered Copernicus and martyred Galileo and disturbing Einstein. Each time, someone had come forth to claim that the new concept diminished man in some way, made him insignificant, infinitesimal, shattered his egocentricity, reduced him to humility. Bud smiled, looked from the alien ship to the Milky Way, and said irreverently:

"What now, oh Lord? Are we not small anymore, or are we smaller than ever? What are we when we've reached the point where the galaxy is a neighborhood?" Bud laughed.

A leafless bush nearby rattled. A dark hulk emerged from behind it, revealing a black hole in the rocky mountainside. Bud leapt to his feet, expecting to confront a coyote, mountain lion or something equally fearsome. There were two creatures: a shorter one followed the first. They were a dark-skinned boy and a dirt-covered dog. The gray short-haired dog seemed to recognize Bud. It barked.

"Ganymede?" Bud hazarded.

She wagged her tail vigorously and jumped up pawing her friend's jacket-waistband. "What are you doing way out here?" Bud asked, bending to greet her; he kept his eyes on the boy - who stood watching. "And who might you be?" he asked the boy. Bud saw from clean lines on his cheeks he had been crying. "Sit, Ganymede, sit . . . atta

193

girl." To the boy, with a smile and a shrug: "I'm just curious."

"Are you Bud Sullivan?"

Bud nodded. "And what's your name?"

"Daren."

Bud waited patiently for the shy boy to tell him more.

"Are you all right?" Daren asked Bud at last.

"So far, so good," Bud answered honestly. "You look a mess. Where have you been?"

The boy pointed to the mountain on the other side of the pass. "I was bringing the dog back."

"Just out for a walk?" Bud asked, noting new tears in the child's eyes. "What did you see?" He looked again in the direction Daren had pointed.

"Home," Daren answered, his voice barely a croak.

Bud's eyes rested on a slot in the mountain; it was on the far side and was amply illuminated by light reflecting from the arroyo. In the slot were only mounds of gray ash; over it on the cliff face were streaks of black soot.

"How many people lived there?" Bud whispered.

"About two hundred. I guess all of them are dead but me."

Bud swallowed. Ganymede, sensing something wrong, whined pitifully. Daren stepped toward Bud, knelt, and stroked Ganymede's neck.

"I had to see," Daren explained, "but—I didn't want to go by myself. The dog—I knew he liked me, so . . .".

"Hungry?" Bud asked.

"I just had one of these," Daren said, showing the wrapper of an instant dinner. "I stole it."

"I don't blame you." Bud felt queazy; he wondered if recent events, and the omnipresence of death, were finally getting to him. Ganymede licked his hand—but he couldn't feel it! Suddenly there was a sharp pain at the back of his skull.

194

"Daren—you know where you got the dog? Would you go back there and bring someone to help me? I think I'm—getting sick."

"I'll help you," the boy said automatically.

"I'm not sure I can walk. I'd be too heavy for you."

Saying nothing more, Daren sprinted away down the mountain and out of sight. Ganymede stayed with Bud.

The moon was the same size as it looked from earth, but in another direction there was the earth itself—full and blue and big, the proverbial marble in the sky. Out still another great window, a brilliant sun brought light and heat and life into Delta Colony.

Bud was standing—almost floating in the one-fiftieth gravity—at one hub of the impossibly huge cylinder, looking down and up at lakes, grassy hills, orchards, clusters of homes and ships, narrow roadways with little electric carts moving silently. In the perennially perfect weather, birds chirped and butterflies flew in colorful clouds.

Another's hand was holding his. Gari stood next to him wearing only wings—like those of a swallow—while Bud felt himself attached to a graceful ribbed kite, like that of DaVinci's winged aeronaut.

They were soaring, banking together, summersaulting, gliding over the inside-out world. Something shot up toward them from the ground. A projectile. Fast. It neared and became distinct: it was William—wingless, his arms extended. Clever William; he could fly without wings. He joined them—Bud on one side of Gari, William on the other. They turned, their backs arched, to make a wide circle all around the cylinder. There were faces at the great windows—ghostly, enormous faces.

Dr. Greitzer was out there in space, looking in. There at another window was Gari's face, next to William's.

And that boy—Daren. Hillary was there too. Bud was not sure he wanted that particular face looking in. Other faces, too—strangers. The faces began to dissolve—not into blackness, as should have been the case, but into a white light. The light was heavy. Bud felt his arms tiring. He might have fallen were it not for the hands that gently took his. The sun began to fade. Night came to the pastoral world below and around him, but no lamps were lighted in the houses. There were stars in the inky blackness.

Finally the stars faded away.

News went out at 5 a.m. that Bud Sullivan was dead of radiation poisoning experienced at the careless hands of the alien visitors. By 9, government, military, and NASA phone channels were jammed with calls of angry, sometimes tearful, protest. The world could forgive numerous anonymous deaths (would probably forgive even the deaths of 200 hill people, though that was not yet known about outside the Twin Peaks camp), but Bud Sullivan was the personal friend of billions. And he had been murdered. Serious retaliatory action was called for— *now*.

Dr. Greitzer arrived at William and Gari's hut at 10:30. He found the two of them at the breakfast table having coffee—ignoring the real-time television image of Jeno and his crew that moved with exasperating slow-motion on a monitor behind them. The sound had been turned off.

"Come in, Doctor," Gari said softly. "Have you had breakfast?"

Greitzer carried a sad expression most of the time; his droopy lids and fallen mouth did not indicate sorrow, did not indicate anything. "Thank you, Gari, but I'm not hungry. I have a number of things to discuss with you both. Time is short." His tone of voice carried meaning not evident on his expressionless face. We knew this would happen, he seemed to say, and now that it has, we must get back to work and reserve our self-pity for a more leisurely time. He pulled up a chair and opened a file folder on the table. He seemed suddenly uncertain what to say first. "I will have some coffee," he tossed off.

"You and I," Greitzer began, "have never seen this operation as military. Others have. William, you should never have spoken to Hal Gordon without obtaining clearance for a press interview from General McCook's office. They're holding Gordon now, detaining him until they decide that it's politic to turn his information loose."

"There's nothing startling in the report I gave him."

"We're talking about a military operation, William—and security, and bureaucracy—not science, not truth. You were in a peculiarly vulnerable position I doubt that you were aware of: that of being practically the only person in the world who could converse with the aliens, and having a free hand to choose your subject matter and method. They were afraid of you, William."

"Were?"

"I have been placed in charge of your operations. I convinced them to assign the job to me not because of my abilities, knowledge, or sympathy with your aims, but because I have often handled military contract projects for NASA. My first task is to persuade you to release the data necessary to make it possible for anyone so inclined to speak directly to the aliens."

"Sure, easy; but that's crazy. In the first place, Gari and I have been in touch with scientists all over the world who are processing our data as fast as we can send it to them. So far, they have all agreed that it is best for one person to be the direct liaison now—simply to avoid confusion. Anybody with a ham TV, a video recorder and computer

197

can do it—and slow up our progress immeasurably."

"I'll tell McCook that. At the moment, he doesn't know it. For now, don't change anything; continue your contacts with them just as you have been doing."

"Get McCook to release Hal Gordon. The public has a right to know the things he can tell them."

Greitzer nodded. "I think we'll even want to add to it. I heard the tape just now, when McCook played it for his staff. McCook is planning—now that the decontamination facility is ready—to 'disarm' the aliens by ordering them to leave their ship. If they don't, you are to tell them, they will be destroyed. If that would be a bad idea, *you* have to talk McCook out of it."

A small dark boy, bare but for underpants, came into the room rubbing his eyes. He said nothing to the adults but went right to the TV monitor and stationed himself in front of it. Ganymede padded in after him and lay down in the middle of the floor.

"He found Bud," Gari said in answer to Greitzer's questioning look. "His name is Daren, but that's all he's told us. He lived at the destroyed hill-people settlement Bud mentioned before losing consciousness."

Greitzer opened the file he had brought with him. "Here are transcripts," he said, ignoring the presence of Daren, "of various semi-reputable statements made to the press concerning your possible complicity with the aliens in some kind of plot against the earth. Here are transcripts from nearly a hundred of the calls NASA has received so far this morning asking for the annihilation of the aliens. I suggest that you—"

"I won't take time to read that nonsense!" William said, apparently bothered that Greitzer would even suggest it.

"You must, William. I won't stand by and see a brilliant man discredited merely because he failed to stand

198

up and say, 'Not guilty.' It's time you joined the inconsistent human race." That ended the topic for Greitzer. He next extracted a single sheet of paper, a photocopy. "This is Bud's will. He drew it up in the hospital and sent me a copy. I'm not sure why he sent it to me rather than to you. Perhaps he hoped I would give you my thoughts about it." He handed it to William.

The significant portion of the will said:

"... and in addition to the list of properties, stocks, and bank accounts, there is one million dollars in credit in my Delta reserve. I leave all of this estate, after the minor debts listed have been paid, to the Starprobe Relay Project headed by Dr. William Reid—in the hope that this gesture will prompt similar and larger contributions in such quantities that the Project can be fully funded privately. It should now be obvious to a great many men of vision that ignorance of the other inhabitants of our galaxy can no longer be tolerated, and that knowledge of the far reaches of space is not only desirable and an exciting prospect, but is necessary to the safety and future well-being of our own world. To William Reid and Gari Copalin personally, I leave all the memories of the times we shared and more love than I knew I was capable of."

Gari and William read it together. William finished and noisily pushed back his chair. He went into the bedroom and closed the door.

Gari had tears in her own eyes, but kept her seat.

"Can you listen to me?" Greitzer asked her.

She nodded.

"NASA has received a number of donations to Starprobe over the last few months. But we returned them—having no administrative procedure alotted to Starprobe any more. We thought the first few were flukes. After I read Bud's will, I called the Houston office and asked them to hold any further contributions for a while.

Last year I would have doubted that the billions necessary could ever in a million years be raised this way. Now I'm not so sure. Talk to William about it. Tell him that not a single contributor has stipulated any decision-making power as a condition."

"That's incredible!" Gari said, sounding as if she had a cold.

Greitzer rose to leave. "General McCook will want to see William this afternoon sometime." At the door, he said, "Oh, I spoke to your father this morning, Gari. He lost his fight. The Senate has ratified the military-preparedness tax surcharge. Daniel is folding his tent and stealing away. He said to tell you that he would be here in a few days."

"Thank you," Gari said.

When Greitzer was gone, she looked into the dark corner where Daren watched the aliens. Something amused the boy. He was laughing.

After a special service, Bud's body was loaded onto a copter to be returned to Dallas for cremation. Hal Gordon (released and allowed to stay at Twin Peaks) handed a sheet of paper to William. While the copter's downdraft tried to rip the paper from his hands, William read that the long-lost second alien ship had been sighted minutes earlier by the observatory at Marginis. The vessel had moved unobtrusively, without a major rocket burn, into the gravitationally stable L-4 point, in the direction from the moon opposite to that of Delta Colony.

Chapter 16

Dark Passage

"Himi," Reno called on the ship's intercom; "we have reached our parking orbit in the gravitational equilibrium point. From here we can receive a great many signals. I can send you different pictures for each of your monitors. Would you like them?"

"Oh, by all means!" Himi responded gaily. "And Reno, can you obtain for me a clear picture of that enormous vessel the aliens are constructing in the other equilibrium point? If you can, put it on the masterscope. I want Fera to contemplate the meaning of it."

"I think I can," Reno said, signing off.

Third-planet studies had become an obsessive pastime for the forcefully retired President. He, with his wife Oado and with the help of his co-husband Reno at the central communications console, had turned exile from the nucleusphere into a happy occasion—an extended much-needed vacation.

Keeping an eye on his six monitors, which were blinking to life, Himi commented to visiting Maoi, "Only someone with the patience of an idiot could enjoy this preoccupation."

Old Maoi laughed. "I know. *I've* always been an idiot, and believe me it's a delight discovering that you're one too." Maoi had (by majority consent) remained behind in the nucleusphere when the scientists and explorers returned to the outersphere.

Himi's political stock among his friends and co-workers was as high now as it had ever been, even though he seldom appeared in the command center and Fera was still in charge. Himi, in fact, was held in almost religious awe: it was said that he could understand the aliens' language! While Fera could guide them to the third planet, only Himi had knowledge of what they would face there.

"Oh look!" said Oado, peering over Himi's shoulder at a monitor. "It's the funny lady—*Paula!*" Oado was laughing even before the comedy had begun.

Himi spoke again to Reno via intercom. "We're not quite down to speed on monitor four. Ah, that's it."

Slowing the images gave the illusion of natural movement to the jerkily hyper-active aliens, but people or objects fell too slowly. The effect was that of a picture in which some actions were normal and others (those involving direct effects of gravity) were in slow motion. Language was processed and slowed to a comfortably understandable rate.

"Poor Jeno," Maoi remarked, seeing the boy-captain's image appear on monitor five. "Is that transmission coming from him, or is it a re-broadcast by the aliens?"

"Reno?" Himi called; "The image on five looks normal. Have you slowed the picture?"

"I've slowed them all."

202

Himi set the intercom box aside. "It's a re-broadcast—sped up by them, slowed down to Jeno's original speed by us."

"If we aren't going to take time to watch the 'Paula' program," Oado pleaded, "be sure to keep the recording of it for later." The comedy was about a bungling lady assistant in a builder's office, whose ineptness resulted in rooms without doors, odd-shaped useless structures, or buildings that had to be hastily propped up to keep them from collapsing. Himi, Oado, and Maoi watched the episodes whenever reception was good enough; they watched as much out of amazement as amusement. The stories seemed preposterously trivial but at the same time psychologically valuable in some way they could not name. While suggesting that the people of the third planet were morons, it also suggested they were admirably kind (forgiving of innocent errors), and intelligent. A fascinating paradox. Most puzzling of all, such programming seemed to have no purpose at all except enjoyment!

A newscast on monitor two showed a helicopter, its rotors moving impossibly slowly, rising from the camp at the site where Jeno's ship had landed. Himi raised the sound level. They heard and understood:

"...transporting the body of (_____) astronaut Bud Sullivan to (_____), where, after a public ceremony, it will be (_____) at the..."

Oado gasped, "He died!"

"I wonder," said Maoi, "if this will be just another death to them, or if it will affect their attitude toward Jeno."

"Can't we help that boy?" Oado asked. "Isn't there some way we can warn him about what Fera plans to do?"

"Not without Fera's knowing we've done it; and that would eliminate any advantage we could give Jeno."

203

"What if," Maoi suggested, "we were to speak to Jeno in the planet's language?"

"Jeno still doesn't understand enough of it," Himi said, shaking his head. "He did not discover how to make the rapid tongue intelligible until after he had landed. He's no further along now than we were a year ago." He added: "Our best course is still to try to stop Fera before it's too late."

Reno's voice came from the intercom: "Himi, I have a picture of the alien's machine on the masterscope. Is that thing as big as it looks? Everybody's just staring at it stupified. Fera wants to talk to you about it; privately, he says."

"Send that picture down to one of our monitors, and ask Fera to come to my apartment."

Maoi looked at Himi quizzically. "What are you up to?"

"You haven't studied the planet for as long as Oado and I have, nor in as great a detail, but from what you have seen, are you certain we would be successful in sending missiles to destroy Jeno's ship where it rests and then in blowing away enough of the planet's atmosphere—that's time consuming, you know—to allow the sun to bake the planet dry and lifeless?"

Maoi thought it over. "Well, their one attempt to strike Jeno down was pretty feeble. They apparently can't break through a simple deflector screen. I suppose we could destroy Jeno's ship easily enough. But as to the rest—only if they're *slow* enough to let us do it at our leisure. They could knock us down eventually—with powerful bombs exploded in our proximity. Unless we could eliminate their striking power at their ground bases. Our one ship would be at war against an entire planet's defenses. Himi, do you hope to convince Fera that however noble, his plan is doomed to failure?"

"Can it hurt to try? If we can plant sufficient doubt in Fera's head—"

"Himi, are you so sure that Fera's plan is unsound? Aren't you letting your affection for your nephew color your thinking?"

"I don't think so, old friend. My concern now is more for that delightful planet down there. Jeno will ultimately have to be destroyed, I'm afraid. But there might be some way to prevent the planet's contamination. As long as no outer seal on Jeno's ship has been broken—"

There was a peremptory knock at the door.

"Come in, Fera," Himi called out in a friendly voice, but Fera was already entering.

"We made it clear to you," Fera began, "that we have no interest in alien broadcasts. Why did you instruct Reno to show us this one?"

"This," said Himi, indicating the appropriate monitor, "is not an alien broadcast. It is a picture from one of our own telecameras."

"Explain," Fera demanded. "You have disrupted our work in the command center. Unfortunately, too many there consider this thing intriguing."

"And you're not intrigued, are you, Fera? Perhaps I ought to help you appreciate the scale of this picture. See that point of light below it there? That is a shuttle carrying more than forty men and women. And there's another similar craft. Does the sight remind you of anything? Of our own boarding of this vessel?"

"But that would mean—"

"That their structure is built along vastly different design principles and is many times the size of ours."

"Are you saying that they will extend themselves into space, as we have done, and will vie with us for habitable planets for colonization? In that contraption?"

"It's their prerogative, isn't it?"

"Then that ship must also be destroyed—which would be a simple matter. The contamination must not be allowed to—"

"What if there is no contamination? What if the citizens of the planet have rescued Jeno and his crew and rendered the ship harmless?"

"You watch their broadcasts. Have they done such a thing?"

"Not yet, but it may be their intention."

"Are you telling me that they could succeed where Hald, and all of our scientists have failed? Are you suggesting that their interstellar ship is superior to ours and that their weaponry might be a danger to us?" Fera was visibly angry. The strain of command had changed him somewhat during his year; he was frequently edgy. "Am I to tell the piloting committee that you have made treasonable and blasphemous statements deliberately to shake our collective confidence? Must we withdraw the privileges you enjoy here in your quarters? Must we instruct Reno to discontinue feeding you alien signals to play with?"

"You make those assumptions, Fera, not I. You must answer their implications for yourself. I felt it my duty to inform you simply that the aliens are capable of constructing such a thing as you see here. You, however, are our President and must lead us according to your own perceptions—or those of your trusted advisors. You said others in the command center wished to know what this enormous piece of equipment is. I trust you will inform them. Is there anything else I can tell you? Anything you are curious about?"

"What do they call their ship?"

"Delta."

"What does that mean? Is it a war-like phrase?"

"I'm not sure. The word in their mathematical vocabulary seems to mean either *third* or *differential*. It probably has other meanings as well. The symbol for it is a triangle."

"There's nothing triangular about this ship's design. It's based on a cylinder, a form *our* designers rejected."

"True."

"What's its means of propulsion. It's compact, apparently; I see nothing there that looks like an engine."

"I don't know."

Fera shook his head condescendingly. "See how useless your hobby is, Himi? The aliens *do not matter*. Only the contamination—the destruction of it—matters. Please have Reno remove that picture from the masterscope."

"I'm sure Reno will comply if *you* ask him."

Fera felt another flush of anger; it showed in his eyes. But he kept his voice ridiculously cordial. "I think it would be best if he heard it from you, Himi. He respects your..." Fera could not finish. He had cornered himself into having to admit that Himi's prestige among certain of his crewmen was greater than his own. Besides, if the order came from Himi, it would reaffirm to the committee that Himi was obliged to obey Fera's orders—or to challenge them publicly and ask for a vote.

Himi smiled. "Certainly," he said. He called Reno and told him: "Remove the picture from the masterscope, and please let the others know that the request came from me, that I am following Fera's orders." Himi's position made it sound as if he were giving Fera permission to play leader for a while longer.

Fera frowned. "You are determined to discredit me. But it will not work." He seemed less than assured of the truth of his assertion.

"I'm sorry, Fera. Isn't that exactly what you wanted me to say and do?" He lifted the intercom. "Would you like me to call again and change the order?"

"I'm having your television connection discontinued and confining you to your quarters," Fera said on his way out the door.

"Very well," Himi responded softly, "but I'll have to request a vote on that."

Exercising great control, a gesture that was wasted on Himi, Fera did not slam the door as he left.

"Will he try it?" Oado asked her husband.

"No," said Himi. "He knows the committee already suspects he has to come to me frequently for advice."

"Does he?" Maoi asked.

"Not really. He's a competent leader, and a very good pilot. His thinking stops short, though; and his intransigence in the face of skimpy evidence is dangerous." Himi watched the monitors—one with its comedy show, another with a children's educational program (these had been extremely helpful to Himi in his early language studies), others with news programs or documentaries, and one with a transmission from Doctor Reid to Jeno. It was this last that held Himi's attention. "Maoi, you have given me an idea. I can't speak secretively to Jeno in the aliens' language, but there is someone to whom I can speak. I'll have to have Fera's permission—his acquiescence at least—because our conversation will take many hours. Come with me. I'll need your support as I lay the situation before the committee and ask for their vote of confidence."

Oado asked excitedly, "Will this restore you to the Presidency?"

Himi chuckled. "I hope not. I want Fera to keep running things for me a while longer. I have more important things to do."

"I don't quite see," Maoi said as they headed for the door, "why you led Fera to believe that the alien machine is a space ship. You once told me you thought it was an artificial domicile. I remember it distinctly because I thought it a brilliant concept, one our people ought to consider."

"Oh? Did I tell Fera it was a ship—one with a mysterious and overwhelming source of power? Careless of me."

"What's the situation?" Pata asked.

"They want us to disembark," Jeno answered. "They have erected some kind of room for us."

"I know *that*," Pata insisted impatiently. "But then what?"

"I—I'm not sure."

"Why isn't Reid the one speaking to us this time?" Eroi asked.

"I don't know," Jeno confessed.

They were watching a stranger who labored to impart information by sign language, photographs, and scattered words that Jeno's party could understand—words he had before him on sheets of paper. While showing pictures of the facility with its long tunnel telescoped, over the water in the crater, to the ship, he repeated a key word a number of times—*safety*.

"We'll have to pass through the outersphere, and—" Eroi began.

"I won't go in there!" Oiro whined fearfully.

"You can go through with me," Jeno offered.

"But," Eroi continued, "we haven't enough vacuum suits. There are only twelve—and sixteen of us. Does that mean that four—?"

Jeno said sternly. "Nobody stays behind. Maybe we won't even need suits, if they have an antidote we can take right away." A thought struck him. "I see what they're doing! Once they have us out, they can enter the ship and

209

clean it with some kind of poison, a gas perhaps."

Eroi objected. "But we'll carry the stuff outside with us—stuck to our space suits or to our bodies."

"I guess they plan to decontaminate us in that place of safety."

"Could it be some kind of trap?" Pata hazarded. "Maybe they want to get us out so they can kill us."

"That's very unlikely, Pata," Jeno said. "If they want to kill us they could blow up the whole ship. I just hope they truly understand the nature of our problem. We showed them many pictures of the gray stuff, but we haven't been able to *tell* them much about it."

"Maybe they recognized it as soon as they saw it. Maybe it's a common thing to them."

"Maybe. Something just occurred to me: we'll have to let air fill the innersphere in order to open the outer hatch. That will probably trigger lots more growth in there, which would clog the machinery. If they aren't able to get rid of the stuff completely, we probably could not re-start the spheres."

"You mean we couldn't take off again?" Eroi asked.

"I'm worrying too much! Surely they are aware of that. Eroi, do you know how to open the outer hatch?"

"I think so. Shall I start programming the machinery?"

"Yes." He instructed Pata: "Go bring me the largest of the space suits. Let's see if two of the smaller of us can get into a single suit."

"Right!"

Eroi seemed troubled by something inconsequential. "I still wonder why Reid isn't the one speaking to us, telling us how to do this. We could understand him a *lot* better."

Jeno shook his head. "I don't know," he repeated.

"Sir, I can't handle this. The way it looks to me, we either shoot them or let them all stay." Colonel Waldrop toyed with his riot gun. "This tranquilizer thing is useless." He was speaking casually and privately to General McCook, in McCook's quarters at Twin Peaks.

"Surely a firm threat—" the General suggested.

Waldrop shook his head. "It's Hillary's mob, sir. They say they have a right to be here, and they're willing to die to prove it. And all those international reporters, nearly 12,000, claim our First Ammendment privileges. As long as they're hanging around, other people think they can too. The CBS guy told me the UN is sending more observers. It's endless. They're coming out of the rocks!"

McCook looked out his window; the sight he had been avoiding drove home the hopelessness of the situation. Humanity had arrived, was still arriving, like the waters of a flash flood. Their campsites and copters stretched across the desert floor to the north as far as the distant mountains. Copters swarmed overhead like insects. Landrovers and hovercraft came in dust clouds over the roadless desert floor arriving like ants to a picnic.

"How come we see the situation as highly dangerous," McCook wondered absently, "and they don't? What do all those millions of people know that we haven't thought of?"

Waldrop suggested wryly, "Ask William Reid."

"I *had* to replace him," McCook said defensively. "He flatly refused to order the aliens to leave their ship. Somebody had to do it."

"Have they agreed to leave it?"

"I don't know."

"I imagine Reid knows."

"Whose side are you on, Waldrop?"

The Colonel laughed. "I'm not sure, sir. But Reid's our expert. Our only expert."

McCook answered a light flashing on his communications link. A voice said, "The demolition men

211

are circling, General; they can't figure out where to land."

Waldrop pointed toward the top of Twin Peaks.

"Have them come down right on top of the mountain," McCook suggested, nodding to Waldrop in appreciation for the suggestion. "We'll send a team up to meet them."

"I've been wondering," Waldrop said when McCook had signed off; "how does one get rid of, well, a hydrogen bomb we can only guess at the yield of? What do you blow it up with? Will *it* be detonated?"

McCook smiled idiotically and shook his head in abject ignorance. "Welcome to Wonderland," he said. "I don't think there's a precedent for this in reality." He added, "Some scientist at the Smithsonian says that if the alien ship blows, she'll take Arizona with her. And part of Mexico." The General got his feet back on terra firma by taking the only concrete action he could think of. He punched a number into his communications link. "I'm calling in the infantry. We've *got* to get all those people away from here."

Waldrop shrugged and nodded. Sounds of distant shouts and cheering reached his ears. I'd better check—"

"You're dismissed," the General agreed; "keep me informed."

Outside, the cheers took on a surrealistic tone: they were begun by a group of protestors at the base of Twin Peaks and then echoed by so many people so far away that it sounded like a howling wind—yet the day was hot and sunny and still. The protestors marched between the NASA camp and the Alienites; they carried banners and placards saying REMEMBER BUD! and SEND 'EM TO KINGDOM COME! and ALIENS GO HOME! Their cheers, evidently, were for the demolition troops descending in familiar brown Army copters to the top of Twin Peaks. Some of the Alienites were arguing loudly,

212

trying to counteract the display of support for destruction; but no violence had broken out between the two groups. So far.

A copter had landed recently on the NASA pad; its rotors were coasting to a stop, making flopping sounds in the air. Waldrop walked toward it, for lack of anything more constructive to do. Senator Copalin stepped out, looked out over the sea of people, mouthed the words, "My God," and was almost instantly surrounded by reporters. Waldrop shoved his way through the knot of shouting questioners.

"Will you try to get Congress to reverse its decision on the surtax?"

"What do you think about the popular movement in support of Starprobe?"

"What do they think in Washington, Senator; is the world in danger of invasion?"

"Are you here to see Dr. Reid?"

They let up long enough to allow the Senator to speak toward their extended microphones and minicameras. "Congress never reverses itself; didn't you know? No, I don't think we're being invaded, and I still think the surtax unnecessary and irresponsible. I'm delighted about Starprobe's support. I intend to support it myself with a contribution. And—what else was it? —oh yes, I am here mainly out of curiosity, just like everybody else; and I do plan to visit Dr. Reid and my daughter."

"What do you know about Hillary's contribution to Starprobe?"

"Probably no more than you do—except perhaps that since Hillary has placed no conditions upon the use of funds, Reid and NASA have tentatively accepted it."

"Know the amount?"

"I don't—sorry."

"What do you think of all these people here?"

"I've never seen anything like it. Have you? What do *you* think of it?"

"Are you here on official business?"

"Unofficially. I've been asked to make a report to Congress, if there is anything to report that isn't already common knowledge."

Waldrop reached the Senator, took his arm, and steered him through the reporters. The Senator followed gratefully but continued to answer questions as he proceeded.

"Are they planning to blow up the space ship?"

"I imagine they are preparing to do so if it proves necessary."

"Are these millions of people going to be allowed to stay?"

"Suicide is no longer a crime in this country. But I think an attempt will be made to at least push the crowds back a number of kilometers."

"Is there imminent danger?"

"That's the first question I have for General McCook and William Reid. I should think you people are better informed now than I am." Colonel Waldrop introduced himself to Copalin and offered to escort him to Reid's hut.

Once inside the hut, Waldrop finally snapped; he couldn't help laughing inanely. The air swarmed with tiny helicopters, a child's model set. The toys buzzed lazily, flying in a pattern of squares as their miniaturized radar, heat-sensors, and transponders directed them to avoid the walls, the furniture, and each other. One came right for his face; Waldrop ducked just as the precision toy made a sharp turn to avoid him.

"They're in the bedroom," said a boy sitting in the center of the floor at a many-levered control box. He

214

added, looking up at Waldrop and Copalin. "It's all right, you can go in."

Waldrop apologized to Copalin. "I guess the situation finally got to me." He laughed again. "I expected to step through the door of this hut into a sensible and intense environment. The toy copters..."

"I understand fully," The Senator said.

"Mr. Hillary gave them to me," the child explained, a little on the defensive.

Copalin raised an eyebrow.

The bedroom also served as a workshop, in case a signal should arrive in the middle of the night. Neither William nor Gari could remember when they had last slept soundly for any length of time.

Waldrop recognized Reid, Gari Copalin, Leon Hillary, Greitzer from NASA, and a man he remembered seeing in TV pictures ordering the aliens to leave their ship; he was Dr. Corothers, the man McCook had brought in to replace Reid. Strange bedfellows, Waldrop thought; he had to concentrate to stifle more silly laughter. Specifically, Hillary, Greitzer, and Gari Copalin were sitting on the bed. Corothers stood against the wall behind them. Reid was sitting close to a monitor with his nose to the screen.

Gari reached out and took her father's hand. No one spoke. They were watching a still picture of a metal-walled room with its furnishings covered in what looked like cobwebs, no, silt—a fine gray mud. An alien's voice could be heard laboriously intoning in a weird language.

"Animal," Gari said. "I think that word means animal. There was no *animal* life on the planet."

"Then why all those big bones in the dig?" Corothers asked. "Perhaps the word means sentient. There was no *sentient* life on the planet."

"No," said Reid. "Animal is the right word. There had been animal life, hence the bones; but none existed at this time. But I can't connect what he's saying with the picture he's showing. Any ideas?"

There were no suggestions. The picture on the monitor changed to that of a view, taken by the aliens, of their own landing sight. The shot came from a camera situated at the equator of their ship, aimed down, showing the decontamination structure.

"I didn't catch a single word of that," Corothers admitted.

"Something about safety precautions," Reid said. "And a repeat of the statement that they are in some kind of difficulty."

The screen went blank. Reid turned to face his companions. "Don't you see the implication? Want me to play it again? Hello, Senator."

"You're telling us what, that the aliens have some kind of plague aboard?" Hillary asked.

Reid nodded. "Something even they can't handle. And they're afraid our decontamination quarters won't be sufficient either. They aren't gods, Hillary. I think they believe *we* are the superior race, or hope that we are, and have come to us for help." He added: "I don't know what's going to happen, but I want you to get your people away from here."

"Even though our alien friends need help," Hillary challenged.

Waldrop asked Reid, on McCook's behalf, "Do you think they will have to be destroyed?"

"Perhaps. I'm morally certain that they should not yet leave their ship. For *our* sake."

"Have you told McCook this?" Waldrop asked.

"Yes. He fired me. I brought Hillary and Corothers here to convince them to add their opinions to mine."

216

Reid looked at each of the two gentlemen in turn." Have I succeeded?"

"I'm afraid not," Corothers said. "I do see that the aliens are concerned for some reason about contamination—whether ours or theirs, I can't tell. I feel obliged to try some convincing of my own, William. That decontamination facility is the finest. If we seal off the tunnel right at their hatch, not even a virus is going to escape. Or enter. And surely you see McCook's military perspective on the thing. He's got to get those aliens away from their source of power. I know Hillary here still thinks they are messengers from heaven, and you seem convinced they are not hostile toward us, but McCook can't take any risks. We've seen how much destructive power they have at their disposal. The only way to disarm them is to get them out in the open. We're not talking about massacring them, for Christ's sake. They'll even have their own air to breathe in our chamber. And we have a complete communications setup for them there, so you can continue your dialog with them. You can have that job, incidentally. I'll tell McCook that you're vastly more qualified than I."

Hillary had his say: "William, they don't *think* like we do. I'm not so arrogant as to believe I could understand them. When they see we're beginning to accept them, they will make their purposes known to us. It's plain useless to try to second-guess intelligences like theirs. They're not about to do anything foolish. If they come out, it will be because they want to and know it's right. If they don't - well, we just wait."

William shook his head. "Who do you suppose made your gods, Leon?" he asked sadly.

"I don't follow you."

"You assume we did not evolve without their help. Who do you suppose helped *them* evolve? And who came

217

along to help their helpers? Do you suppose there was ever, in the universe, a species of intelligent beings who made it on their own?"

"On that note of nonsense," Hillary said, rising from the bed, "I leave you to ponder your own paradoxes. We've got a big meeting tonight, and I need to grab a little shut-eye to get my energy up."

When Hillary was gone, Senator Copalin commented pensively, "There goes the most dangerous man alive."

"And the most frightened," Greitzer added. "His kind are so afraid of life and the realities of earth, that they feel more at home with an imaginary alien perspective. Their Eden is anywhere but here."

Waldrop said gravely, "Dr. Reid, you have my support—which is probably not worth much." He had his hand on the doorknob. "I'll go see if McCook will listen to me." As he exited he added: "Don't get your hopes up."

That evening, just before sunset. Jeno's ship was shaded by the western mountains; bluish floodlights were being turned on for the demolition team. Hillary and his followers were sharing their beliefs, their hopes for a dazzling future of technological perfection; they were spread over the north mountain, where once 200 hill people had eked out a meager agrarian existence. The Alienites faced the miraculous alien sphere.

Hillary was at the base of the mountain in a focal point of the crowd. He spoke into his phone; the multitude listened with their own instruments tuned to receive him. He spoke of Mayan ruins, the Pyramids, Atlantis—a complex mythology linked to a benevolent galactic intelligence with a purpose for mankind.

Suddenly there was a burst of static, then a persistent hiss, then a voice. The sound was in a man's baritone register, but it was inhuman—like the too-perfect voice of a computer. There was an accent—like German, someone remarked—but the diction was sharp enough to prevent misunderstanding. It said:

"Pardon interrupting. Most urgent you do not require Jeno to leave the ship. Most dangerous to your planet. Please request to converse with Reid. Request to use 231.7 channel. Speak in your own language. My name is Himi."

The message was not repeated.

Although the message had been carried on dozens of frequencies and was heard the world over, many of those on the mountainside stared at their phones dumbfounded, feeling that a great alien presence had chosen to participate in their twilight ceremony.

Hillary, without a word, turned his back to the crowd, stretched out his arms and began to walk toward the ship. His followers followed. Guards simply stepped aside; they felt helpless to stop the advancing wall of arms and legs, and eyes that had seen the truth.

When he reached the crater's edge, Hillary took a phone from his pocket and addressed his people: "If the government intends to destroy this ship, let them destroy all of us as well. Here we are, and here we shall stay." Replacing the phone in his pocket, Hillary—standing beside a bewildered security guard who held a riot gun limply at his side—knelt on the earth, sneaked a glance upward to be sure he was directly beneath one of Jeno's cameras, and spread back his arms in a chest-bearing gesture clearly imparting: do with us what you will.

Demolition men wearing protective suits were standing knee-deep in the crater pool, watching. When it was clear that Hillary's people intended to advance no farther, the men returned to their work: attaching large packages of non-nuclear explosives to the underbelly of the sphere.

A little before midnight, word reached the arroyo that Reid had been given a clear channel, all over the world, and was in touch with the alien called Himi.

Early the next morning, Hal Gordon tossed a phone through an open window of Reid's hut. His plaintive voice came through it: "Help! What's happening? Can't you tell us something?"

Gari stepped outside an hour or so later and told the restless hoard of reporters sitting on the dusty ground that Himi was in the other alien ship in the L-4 region, that Reid was in touch both with Himi and with Jeno in the arroyo, that plans were being worked out, and that due to the complexity of the communications procedure there was simply no way Reid could take the time to provide a translation of what had transpired so far.

"When can we have a full translation?" a woman asked.

Gari shrugged. "When it's all over, I guess."

Hal Gordon roved among the observers collecting man-on-the-street comments for the New York Times and the Times TV Syndicate. Among the Alienites, he gathered:

"Good morning. Well, don't you feel it too? Importance in the air—like ozone."

"No matter what happens here today, none of us will ever be the same again. Our experience together, the love millions of us are sharing, the sense of belonging to the universe and the ages... will stay with us forever."

"It's intoxicating to risk your life for a principle."

Among the unaffiliated observers, Gordon recorded:

"Why do people run to see a fire? I just wanted to see it."

"I want to tell my grandchildren I was there when a new concept of a populated galaxy was born. It's not the same staying home to watch it on TV."

"I like to speculate. Those people have been to other

star systems and other planets with strange forms of life. They are a pretty strange form of life themselves. I like to sit here and listen to all the reports and wonder what the aliens are thinking about *us*."

Gordon stopped a group of "Remember Bud" demonstrators who were boarding a copter. One of them told him:

"We're leaving. We did what we came to do, and we're more or less satisfied that General McCook doesn't plan to let the creeps get away with murder. It's all over but the big bang anyway. We're just trying to beat the exodus out of here."

And there was an exodus. The following evening, McCook warned that anyone left in the camp fourteen hours later was sure to be killed.

Hillary's group steadfastly refused to budge. They ate truckloads of hamburgers and sang camping songs.

An horrendous rumbling sound echoed through the arroyo. Many in Hillary's multitude stood up, worried, and looked to their leader.

"Do you want to believe they would kill us?" Hillary asked rhetorically. But he understood the sound, as did many others. Jeno had begun the turning of his internal centrifugal mechanisms.

Few if any of the Alienites slept that night. They listened to the slow climbing in pitch of the alien machinery.

Gari Copalin, at around two in the morning, ran to Hillary and handed him a sheet of paper. On it, Reid repeated McCook's warning and stressed that the aliens supported the inevitability of grave danger. Hillary's resolve was shaken somewhat, but still he refused to move. "We have to know why," he told Gari.

Near dawn, when the sky was just bright enough to indicate a cloudless day to come, Reid called Hillary on the phone. "Set up your public address channel, Leon," he requested. "Someone wishes to speak to you."

Himi's mechanized voice rose from the million phones in the arroyo:

"Leon Hillary, Himi is speaking to you. Reid and I have found some solutions, but the situation is difficult. I personally ask that you and your people abandon your position. Move many many kilometers away, and do it quickly. Jeno and I are deeply grateful for your concern, but there is no more you can do."

As they made their orderly exit through the pass, the Alienites saw that the NASA camp was no longer there behind Twin Peaks—except for two huts, Reid's and McCook's. There were very few lights out on the north desert floor where a few days ago there had been a transient city. The demolition team swam frantically through their midst, hurrying back into the arroyo.

By dawn the area was deserted.

There were no campsites, no copters, no aircraft, no ground vehicles; no sign of life aside from the alien sphere.

Acute sun rays broke over the top of Twin Peaks and brightened the top of the sphere.

Large gold and purple flowers—where a month ago there had been only ashes—moved gently in a dry breeze.

The water still remaining in the crater quivered—it had a surface like stucco—from the vibrations carried to it by the ship's landing legs.

Remote telescopic cameras showed the world the final event: the water in the basin suddenly evaporated; flowers were torn of at their roots and blown away; a light dimmed up to illuminate the arroyo from within; the light beneath the sphere became a sun; the sphere rose slowly from the ground; the brightness became so great that every camera's picture was washed white; out of the white

222

a round shadow made a brief appearance; the hint of movement around it were landing legs being retracted; the white again consumed any trace of picture as the ship rose higher and was eclipsed by its own propelling fire; a wide-angle picture of the desert and the sky showed a daytime star streaking up toward the blue-purple zenith.

An alien voice that did not sound like Himi's interrupted every broadcast momentarily. "Thank you," it said.

Chapter 17

Triangulation

A world accustomed to instantaneous on-the-spot news coverage found the unknowns from Arizona intolerable. Who were the aliens? Why had they come? What did Reid say to them? Had the earth been in danger? Was it still in danger? Were the aliens in danger? Could they speak in English? And so on. The press obligingly supplied partial answers and guesses from people willing to provide them—as long as the providers had famous names or reasonably good reputations in some realm of scientific endeavor.

It was a full three days after Jeno's departure, however, before any "inside" information became available. Early headlines proclaimed that William Reid had prepared a videotape of the inter-species conversation; since the conversation involved two languages and a peculiar difference in speech patterns, the edited tape had to be translated and electronically processed before it could be released for general consumption. Hal Gordon managed to scoop all global services by obtaining a translation scribbled in Reid's longhand. It was a hasty voiceprint which was disseminated in a "extra" to subscribers of the Times—several hours before the first of many TV broadcasts of Reid's tape.

The Times transcription was not as complete as the later TV tape, but it served to answer many questions and posed others to be answered in the centuries to come. For subscribers whose home or office receivers printed out on paper (it was different for microfilm or CRT display), the story began on page one with a set of explanations:

● Tedious exchanges about transmission procedures have been omitted.

● Requests for repeats for the sake of clarification have also been omitted.

● Mathematical information has been omitted or simplified.

● Alien words for which precise definitions were lacking appear in brackets indicating that the translation is likely valid but is in some doubt.

● Inarticulate English words used by the aliens are also inferred and bracketed.

● A more trustworthy and complete transcription, which Dr. Reid himself has agreed to edit, will be published at a later date.

Himi - Has Jeno left his ship?

Reid - No.

Himi - Is his lock to be opened?

Reid - Yes, although Jeno seems reluctant to do it. Explain.

Himi - There are a thousand dead in Jeno's ship. They

died from [ingesting] a living substance that is [sub-cellular] and for which we have found no preventive. Jeno and the children live only as long as they are isolated in the center of the sphere protected by a vacuum immediately [surrounding them]. If they pass through the contamination they die. If they carry the infection onto your planet, your planet dies.

Reid - Your last message has been repeated to our commander here. He will prevent Jeno's disembarkation. Why did Jeno land here?

Himi - I believe they thought your civilization so far in advance of ours that you might succeed in saving them where we have failed. I believe they felt invited by your man Hillary.

Reid - How does it happen that Jeno's crew are children?

Himi - [Courageous] and heroic children. Their parents were the ship's pilots who died voluntarily and had set the ship to destroy itself. Jeno, an adolescent, took possession of the ship with assistance of older ones from the nursery. My brother was President and is among the dead. Jeno is his son.

Reid - Are you President of your ship? Do you have a plan to save Jeno?

Himi - I am President. I have no plan. I see by your asking that you realize Jeno's ship must be destroyed. We hope to entice Jeno into space and destroy him there. In this you must help. Jeno will not accept transmissions from my ship because he believes, with reason, that we are his enemies. First we appeal to his sense of honor. I do not believe he knows the extent of damage he did at the time of his landing. Will you give him the count of your dead?

Reid to Jeno - (omitted)

226

Reid to Himi - I have done as you requested. There was no reply. Why could not Jeno live out his life aboard his ship awaiting a time when a solution can be found? A scientist here, Greitzer, asks if you have considered laboring to peel away the ship's layers—in space, where the lethal substance would be killed?

Himi to Reid - Tell Greitzer this was our best plan and the last we considered. We voted that such an action would have a fair chance for success. But if only the smallest particle survived in, for example, the warm fold of a space suit, we would all suffer eventually. Further, the procedure would consume perhaps a year of work. Time we do not have. Our home planet can exist only a few more generations before it [becomes] too hot to be habitable. We must find other planets that have no dominant intelligent species, to which our people can [immigrate]. The existence of a planet-killer such as lives on Jeno's ship is [abhorrent] to us.

Reid to Himi - What if Jeno's whereabouts and state of health were always known to you?

Himi to Reid - Perhaps you do not appreciate the distances we cover. We could not burden our mission with maintaining uninterrupted line of sight with Jeno's ship.

Reid to Himi - Permit me to converse with Jeno. Please supply translations into your language of the following words. (list omitted)

Reid to Jeno - We now understand the problem you hoped we could solve. We cannot. If your air lock were opened, our planet would be endangered. We admire you for what you have attempted and consider the deaths you caused unintentional. But you must leave. How long do you require to prepare for departure? We must clear your area of our people.

Reid to Jeno - Did you receive my messages? Please respond. I will repeat them. (repetition omitted)

Jeno to Reid - Received. Please tell what Himi [plans to do] with us.

Reid to Himi - Should I tell him the truth?

Himi to Reid - No. He might attempt to evade us and might succeed.

Reid to Jeno - I have an idea that might help you. It will require consultation with other scientists and will take time. Please begin your lift-off procedures. We can continue to converse after you are in space.

Jeno to Reid - We will depart in fourteen hours [according to] your [measurement of time].

Himi to Reid - I wait to hear more.

Himi to Reid - Where are you?

Jeno to Himi - He endeavors to save us, Uncle.

Himi to Jeno - Beloved Jeno! You understood my words in the alien language! Have you listened? Have you understood all that Reid and I have said?

Jeno to Himi - No.

Himi to Jeno - Are you well? Are the children well? Answer in the alien language.

Jeno to Himi - Frightened. You [permit] us escape? Why do fear [overheard]? Who?

Himi to Jeno - There is still time. We must talk about many things, Jeno. Even happy things!

Reid to Himi and Jeno - If you have watched our broadcasts for the past year, you may have learned about our Starprobe Relay Project. It is to be an unmanned series of probes to be sent through what we believe might be an inhabited sector of the galaxy. The sections are to be launched a year apart. It seems now that our first probe will be launched in about a year and a half. I propose that Jeno leave now and serve as the leader of that team of probes. If he adheres to the schedule of trajectories and course maneuvers we can supply, we will be aware of his location at all times. He would make no landings. Jeno's reports could be transmitted both to us and to your home planet. We could relay them if necessary. Your people need not suffer the total loss of one of its vitally needed explorers. Are there sufficient facilities in Jeno's sphere for the constant replenishment of air and food supplies? Have you a closed and recycling ecology?

Himi to Reid - All of that is possible. But a [paramount] concern remains. If Jeno's crew should die, how to prevent the ship's being a derelict that could crash or be boarded?

Reid to Himi - Is it possible for Jeno to install a device that could cause the ship to destroy itself if no sign of life is detected for a certain period of time?

Himi to Reid - [exclamation] There is one already existing system which might be adjusted to perform such a function. A scientist and friend, Maoi, is considering it.

Jeno to Himi - Too much alien words. Please explain me plan you and Reid discuss.

Himi to Jeno - I will send you instructions later.

Himi to Reid - Has Jeno begun the rotation of his spheres?

Reid to Himi - Yes.

Himi to Reid - Are your observers away from the ship?

Reid to Himi - Hillary's group refuses to leave, believing their presence protects Jeno from hostile actions by us. Will you speak directly to them?

Himi to Hillary - (omitted)

Reid to Himi - Can we not exchange information? We would like to know the location of your planet, what life there is like—in greater detail than Jeno supplied—and we would like to know which star systems you have visited and what you found there.

Himi to Reid - Certainly. And there is much you can

tell us. From our [outsider's] point of view, yours is an [unaccountably] successful planet. What functions do your governments serve? What is the need for television stories such as "Paula"? Most important, will you send [blueprints] of Delta Colony? Such a domicile might mean at least temporary salvation for my planet.

Reid to Himi - To us, our world has not always seemed a happy place. The governments which have dominated in one age or another have been based on three principles: privilege for an elite, privilege for the collective, and freedom for the individual. We can send you a lifetime of study on the subject. "Paula" is just an entertainment. We can surely send you Delta blueprints and will be happy if they are of practical use.

Himi to Reid - The self-destruct mechanism you proposed is [practicable], but there is a faction aboard this ship voting strongly for destruction here and now, nevertheless. They do not trust the children to be willing or able to make the necessary commitments. Is there an escape route Jeno might take?

Reid to Himi - If Jeno can remain hidden from you by our planet for a time, and then propel himself at high speed toward the sun—there to use solar gravity to sling him along his prescribed Starprobe course—would this permit his escape? I send coordinates in my language; I sense the need. (math omitted)

Himi to Reid - Yes.

Reid to Jeno - Stand by to receive instructions for orbit and departure.

Jeno to Himi - Please explain what is happening!

Himi to Jeno - Reid is your guide into space. At the moment, your life is in his hands.

Jeno to Himi and Reid - We launch in minutes. We fear we die. We fear sleep soon. But we must say to planet.

Himi to Reid - We seem better equipped to interrupt your normal communications frequencies. Will you forgive our doing it one more time? May I relay Jeno's message?

Reid to Himi - Yes.

Jeno to Himi to the Earth - Thank you.

Himi to Reid - For now, I have [shifted] blame for Jeno's escape to you. There is [pandemonium] aboard my ship, but it will subside. And many are as relieved as I. Is Jeno on course?

Reid to Himi - Jeno is on course. Do you trust the boy to do what must be done?

Himi to Reid - Yes. He is like his father. Others will never be convinced, however, and we must live with that [loneliness]. We have plotted the first leg of our next venture. Stand by for the reception of those numbers (omitted). We can remain in communication for several years. Also within the numbers you can find the location of our planet. You will see that we are not quite neighbors. I have begun our departure sequence.

Reid to Himi - I feel that friends are leaving me.

Himi to Reid - I feel that also.

Reid to Himi - You and I have placed the fate of the galaxy into the hands of children.

Himi to Reid - Is not the future always in the hands of children? With us, responsibility often follows the feeling that one is trusted. I must sleep.

Reid to Himi - So must I.

A PASSION FOR HONOR
Louise MacKendrick

LB467KK $1.75
Nonfiction

Jackson Devereaux had nothing but his rifle and a powerful sense of mission when he came out of the Everglades determined never to return. They called him "swamp-trotter" and other names—but never to his face. Because to insult him was to ask for sudden death. "King Jack" built his private kingdom, sired sons and daughters, but that was only the beginning. For when a man is king there are those who seek to topple him from his throne.

PLEASURE IS OUR BUSINESS
Jack Sandberg

LB468KK $1.75
Nonfiction

This is an explosive exposé of America's fastest growing, profit-making industry, the *total* relaxation center. Sandberg investigates Manhattan's expensive sex clubs . . . establishments that cater to the needs of the "establishment" . . . bars, restaurants, music, topless and bottomless young women in a variety of decors from the decadence of the Roman Empire to the pageantry and pomp of the Indian mosque. Whether cash or charge, anything could be had for a price.

BLOODY GRASS
Hobe Gilmore

LB469DK $1.50
Western

The U.S. Cavalry was busy with booze, squaws, and officers' wives. But Redband, the crazed renegade Sioux was on the warpath and would stop at nothing to have revenge on white men . . . and white women.

TARK AND THE GOLDEN TIDE
Colum MacConnell

LB470DK $1.50
Fantasy

Usurped heir to the throne of the Tumbling Cliffs, Tark and his mentor Morned the Flea journey from the town of Sorne to the Silver Mountains transporting the coveted blue sapphire that is the fabled gem of luck for the Sornese. This is Tark's journey: past the beasts of the Burning Wood, the pirates of the Shallow Sea, and the Princess of the Silver Mountains. But there, at journey's end he must mount his giant fighting camel and meet his deadliest foe—the usurper Akor-Lut, Warmaster of the Golden Tide.

BLOOD MONEY
Aaron Fletcher

LB471DK $1.50
Western

Bounty hunter Jake Coulter is back as he scours the west for outlaws with a price on their heads. Now they would know how it felt to be a hunted animal.

THE WICKED WYNSLEYS
Alanna Knight

LB472DK $1.50
Gothic

Mab Wynsley and her young actor fiancé buy a mansion as their future home. Until the marriage she would live there accompanied by her sister . . . but soon the house of hope is smashed and she finds herself, her sister, and her future husband actors on a stage of death.

Cherry Delight
THE DEVIL TO PAY
Glen Chase

LB473DK $1.50
Adventure

Cherry Delight is sent to France to investigate a cult of devil worshippers—extortionists who murder, rape, and maim for pleasure and profit. The Devil presided over the Black Mass and orgies. But he and his disciples were in for a surprise . . . they had never seen hell until Cherry arrived.

PRIME TIME

James Kearney

LB499-2 $1.95

Novel

The book that picks up where *Network* left off . . . The explosive novel of violent power struggles inside a giant television network. The United Television Network. Outside an austere glass facade . . . inside a seething hot bed of ambitious men and women whose motto was "show your rivals no mercy" . . . men and women who would get what they wanted at any cost. (Foil cover)

FLAME IN A HIGH WIND

Jacqueline Kidd

LB500-X $1.50

Adventure

A Powerful novel of romance and adventure on the high seas. The War of 1812 ended for all but Capt. Denny Poynter. Branded pirate, pursued by British and Americans alike, he fought and plundered his way around the world. But his reckless freedom would be soon jeopardized as his first lady, the sea, gave way to the fiery Renee.

THAT COLLISION WOMAN

Deidre Stiles

LB501-8 $1.95

Novel

Fleur Collison was known as the most beautiful and wilful woman in all England. The young English-woman would return to her ancestral home of Ravensweir despite the fact that it was inhabited by her former lover, now brother-in-law. She was determined to take what she wanted from the world . . . and her sister.

ELENA

Emily Francis

LB502-6 $1.50

Mystery

The commune on this small Greek island lived a placid life among ancient monuments and clear blue sea until Elena came. They gave her friendship and love. She brought them death.

HOW TO DIVORCE YOUR WIFE
Forden Athearn

LB503-4 $1.95
Nonfiction

Practical advice for men from an experienced divorce lawyer, Forden Athearn on what to do before you tell your wife, how to tell your wife, family, boss, how to select a lawyer, and more!

DAY OF THE COMANCHEROS
Steven C. Lawrence

LB504-2 $1.50
Western

Slattery had witnessed the rape, murder, and pillage by the savage Comancheros but it wasn't personal until they put him on the end of a rope. No one dared stop them. Someone had to.

KILLER SEE, KILLER DO
Jonathan Wolfe

LB505-0 $1.50
Mystery

It started out as an innocent Halloween party. But innocent soon turned to bizarre when the treats stopped and a trick involving voodoo brought death to the scene. Someone was jailed and Indian detective Ben Club meant to set him free.

GUNSMOKE
Wade Hamilton

LB506-9 $1.50
Western

Ben Corcoran had become boss of Sageville range by killing anyone who tried to settle. When the quiet gambler came to town no one took notice . . . until he led the farmers in bloody revolt. First Time in Paperback.

ANNA
Dagfinn Grönoset

LB458DK $1.50

Non-fiction

In her eighties, an extraordinary Norwegian woman tells of how, fifty years ago, she was sold into lifelong bondage, of her struggles to support her masters and herself in a mountain wilderness, and of her own triumphant survival as a human being. Originally published by Knopf.

ONLY ON SUNDAY
Linda DuBreuil

LB459DK $1.50

Non-fiction

Here are true stories about one small town's principal figures—the preacher with a past who deserts his wife and runs off with the parish funds, the church deacon and the pianist who carry on an affair made in heaven, and a host of others who feign morality six days a week only to sin on the seventh! A paperback original.

SATAN'S MANOR
Mark Andrews

LB460KK $1.75

Novel

The movie crew came to the decaying mansion to film its story . . . a legend filled with murder, revenge, death. The project was jinxed from the beginning with injury, accidental deaths, and strange events. But what would happen soon would be more horrifying than any special effects man could create! A paperback original.

BOUNTY HUNTER
Aaron Fletcher

LB461ZK $1.25

Western

The Bounty Hunter Series will follow the exploits of Jake Coulter, a ruthless bounty hunter determined to bring his prey in dead or alive . . . at any cost. It is a fast paced, fierce, and realistic western ablaze with all the elements that have made our *Sundance* Series an all time bestseller! A paperback original.

THE LIFE OF KIT CARSON   **LB474ZK $1.25**
John S.C. Abbott   **Golden West Series**

Christopher "Kit" Carson was a legend to his countrymen. Trapper, trailblazer, scout, and Indian fighter, Kit Carson would become part of American history at its most exciting time—the pioneering of the wild west.

THE YOKE AND
THE STAR   **LB475TK $1.95**
Tana de Gamez   **Novel**

"This tense, compassionate novel has an animal warmth and female ferocity that is very moving indeed."

—Kirkus Review

"Expert story-telling, excitement and suspense."
—Publishers Weekly

Cuba was ready to explode into bloody revolution. Hannan, the American newsman, could feel the tension in the air, in the eyes of the people in the streets and cafes. Everybody was taking sides; there could be no neutrals in the coming conflict. Hannan thought he could stay out of it. He was wrong. Love for a beautiful revolutionary pushed him past the point of no return.

THE RETURN OF
JACK THE RIPPER   **LB476KK $1.75**
Mark Andrews   **Novel**

An English acting company opened a Broadway play based on the bloody Ripper murders of 1888. Just as the previews began, a prostitute was found dead in a theatre alley—disembowelled, her throat slashed. Other murders followed, and soon the city was gripped in terror. Had the most monstrous figure in the annals of crime returned to kill again?

THE RED DANIEL
Duncan MacNeil

LB477DK $1.50
Adventure

The Royal Strathspey's, Britain's finest regiment, are dispatched to South Africa to take command in the bloody Boer War and find the most fabulous diamond in all of South Africa—The Red Daniel.

SLAVE SHIP
Harold Calin

LB478KK $1.75
Adventure

This is the story of Gideon Flood, a young romantic who sets sails on a slave ship for a trip that would change his life. He witnesses the cruelty of African chieftains who sell their own for profit, the callousness of the captains who throw the weak overboard, and his own demise as he uses an African slave and then sells her.

A SPRING OF LOVE
Celia Dale

LB479KK $1.50
Novel

"A fascinating story."

—The Washington Star

"An immaculate performance . . . unsettling, and quite touching."

—Kirkus Review

This sweeping novel chronicles a determined young woman's search for enduring love. No matter where it took her, she followed her heart. The man with whom she linked her fortunes was said to be dangerous, but she knew there could be no one else.

TIME IS THE SIMPLEST THING
Clifford D. Simak

LB480DK $1.50
Science Fiction

Millions of light years from Earth, the Telepathic Explorer found his mind possessed by an alien creature. Blaine was a man capable of projecting his mind millions of years into time and space. But that awesome alien penetrated his brain, and Blaine turned against the world . . . and himself.

SEND TO: LEISURE BOOK
P.O. Box 270
Norwalk, Connecticut 06852

Please send me the following titles:

Quantity	Book Number	Price
_____	_____	_____
_____	_____	_____
_____	_____	_____
_____	_____	_____
_____	_____	_____

In the event we are out of stock on any of your selections, please list alternate titles below.

_____	_____	_____
_____	_____	_____
_____	_____	_____
_____	_____	_____

Postage/Handling _____

I enclose . . . . . . _____

FOR U.S. ORDERS, add 35¢ per book to cover cost of postage and handling. Buy five or more copies and we will pay for shipping. Sorry no C.O.D.'s.

FOR ORDERS SENT OUTSIDE THE U.S.A.
Add $1.00 for the first book and 25¢ for each additional book. PAY BY foreign draft or money order drawn on a U.S. bank, payable in U.S. ($) dollars.

☐ Please send me a free catalog.

NAME_____
(Please print)

ADDRESS_____

CITY _____ STATE _____ ZIP _____
Allow Four Weeks for Delivery